Tell Me

the

Truth

Tell Me the Truth

Love, the Enemy Series: Book One

SOFIE DAVES

ISBN-13: 9798397596572 (paperback)

Cover design by: Sofie Daves

www.SofieDaves.com

Printed in the United States of America

My reason for everything ...

The beginning, the middle, and our X, Y, and Z

Table of Contents

Prologue

Alexandra

Wednesday

Having to say goodbye to Ellis after the movies was so hard. As I watched him drive away, I was very hot and bothered and felt a bit mad at him for not coming inside with me to finish what we started. By myself in my house, I started thinking about what we were doing when we were alone in the movie theatre.

Ellis kissing me felt incredible. I could suck on his candy mouth all day. The way he started his hand at the back of my neck and moved his fingers up under my hair, along my scalp. Then when he clenched his fingers to take hold of my hair, gently yet firmly, my senses were going crazy. That feeling of being controlled with my head held so that he could kiss me any way he wanted, was wildly exciting.

His hot breath in my ear, was moist and deep, and when he whispered, "I want to feel you," I was ready to drop my inhibitions and fulfill all his fantasies, and mine. I can still feel how my only available reaction was some sort of moan or gasp or gulp since my senses were tangled in a mess of lust, wanton, and desire. There were no words for what I wanted him to do with me.

The feel of his rough hands under my clothing and along my skin. Easily bringing my nipples to attention. The thought of what could have happened if another couple hadn't entered the theatre…

As I'm walking upstairs and getting ready for bed, I then start thinking about the events earlier in the day, trying to play out if something happened that made Ellis want to leave, instead of joining me here inside. We laughed tirelessly all day, so much so that I let my guard down and even forgot about my worries back at work.

"I hope I can see you again tomorrow." He said before he got back into his car and drove off.

It has taken my body and mind a bit to cool down after parting with Ellis. Only now am I starting to feel rational and possibly believe that he did want to stay, just as much as I wanted it.

It's just sexual frustration, I assure myself. *We're both busy people. We have our businesses to answer to.* Instead, I allow myself to be positive, present, and thoughtful. After all, I feel lighter than I have in months.

I'm starting to feel something real for this man. *This could work*, I think to myself before I drift off to sleep, starting to dream about Ellis.

***

5:00 a.m. My alarm and the aroma of coffee wake me up from deliciously naughty dreams that I don't remember but can still feel deep within my body.

With my head on my pillow, I reach over to stop my alarm and quickly glance over at my phone, resting on my bedside table. No messages, so I undress and hop into the shower. The soothing water and fresh scent of body wash, shampoo, and conditioner gather my senses into an eddy of contentment, exhilaration, and anticipation. There's a lot to look forward to with Ellis, even if we have to balance our new relationship with the demands at work.

Before leaving my house, it's my daily morning habit to pause and acknowledge my favorite picture of my mom hung on the wall across from the door that goes to my garage. Her head is set against a background of muted greens of grass and trees. The park, the forest, and even the garden at our home were her favorite places. When this picture was taken, it was a beautiful sunny day.

My mom's dark hair flowed to her shoulders in waves as she looked lovingly, and with a bit of mischief, at the photographer – my dad. Her expressive grey eyes reach back with love. Her grey eyes are my own -- the part of her I get to carry with me every moment of every day.

"Almost there, Mom," I whisper to her picture, one version of the same secret I tell her each morning.

It is just before 6:30 a.m. when I arrive at the office and, as usual, I am the first one here. I head directly to the lab and my heart jumps for joy when I see that there has been a break in my research. A note from my assistant reads: *I've been trying to contact you. Take a look at these results.*

The goal of our research is to develop various antibody and/or nucleic acid therapies for treating cancer, autoimmune and infectious disorders with the intention of lessening or removing drug dependency. If my hunch is right, I have developed a novel immunotherapy, vaccine-type treatment that can be used for many chronic illnesses, including cancer.

It takes me just over an hour to look over the readings on my tablet. While there were varying effects on target cells in initial tests, these new tests show complete incapacitation. In addition, levels of toxicity on urine samples for the lab rats show non-existent.

I check and double-check the results against the benchmarks we wanted to reach. It is important to be sure we have successfully achieved what we wanted in our findings.

When I am sure that what I am looking at after rounds of testing and re-testing is exactly what I had hoped for, I roll back in the lab stool and stand up.

Grabbing the edge of the laboratory counter with both hands, I pause and enjoy a rush of accomplishment washing over me. These are the results we've been hoping for.

We can finally move on to the clinical trial stage.

This means more confidence in my company's earning potential both when this therapy goes to trials and then is released, which equates to a jump in stock prices and the investments needed to pay for more research and development.

It also means no more talk of selling shares. For now. I feel a great sense of pride in my work and everything I have built. It is one of those times when I feel humbled by the impact that I can have on the world.

"Thanks for being with me all along, Mom and Grandma," I say, looking up and feeling their love for me. "All this is for you. I love you."

Elated, and wanting to set a time to see Ellis, I grab my phone to text him and share my great news. "Oh gosh, still in Silent mode," I say. I forgot to turn it back on after the movie last night. I flip the switch to turn my phone back to Ring.

Ding. Ding. Ding. Ding. Ding. Ding. Ding. Ding.

When I see that Ellis has texted me, my heart leaps into the highest of elevations. But, as I read up, in reverse time order, through the string of Ellis' text messages, my heart quickly goes from glee to the depths of anger, embarrassment, confusion, and betrayal.

"Just in case you need to reach me. E"

"Please call me. Let me explain."

"Alexandra please."

"Just checking in to see how you're doing. Please call me."

"Called. Left a VM. Please call me back."

"Let me explain. I need to see you."

"I'm sorry. Don't believe everything you hear until we talk. Please."

As I am sitting on the lab barstool, confused and not knowing what to do next, I hear the nearby elevator ding and the doors slide open.

"Alexandra?" I hear my assistant's voice behind me. It sounds softer than usual, almost like she is in some sort of trouble. I turn around, eager to brush away whatever mistake she thinks she might have made so that I can figure out the meaning behind Ellis' text messages.

Seeing my assistant, Tracey, instantly transports me away from Ellis' texts, to what is important: My research.

"What's wrong? Whatever it is, don't worry about it!" I tell her. Happy to forget about the confusion I was feeling just seconds before. "We've waited months for this." Pointing at the results on my tablet. "And waited even longer to maintain the correct ST levels. Great job Tracey!"

Tracey seems to be searching my eyes, which is strange since I think it's obvious that I am pleased with the results of our research. I am ready to offer her a pep talk of some sort, but then I see her expression change to realization. She suddenly grasps that we're not talking about the same thing.

I don't know what she knows.

"I assume you haven't seen…you must not know yet…" She starts to speak, with the same hushed, tentative voice. She swipes up on her phone and thumbs to the screen she wants to show me. She walks to me with her phone in hand and says, "I think you need to see this."

"What is it?" I question her, as I accept her phone and focus my eyes on the screen.

The picture on Tracey's phone screen is of a man in a leather jacket and a baseball cap with a woman by his side. She is wearing jeans, a cropped jacket, and a baseball cap. I would have dismissed the picture, but then a flash of recognition sticks in my mind, and I look closer, recognizing both outfits. It is Ellis' jacket and the same white, cropped one that I wore last night. I scroll down through the article and find another picture.

Apparently, Ellis and I were followed. Anger rises within me, knowing that I was photographed, despite my efforts to stay incognito.

But these pictures don't seem like enough to ruin my day. Until my mind recalls the flood of emotions that had surged moments before Tracey arrived. Puzzle pieces start forming connections.

"Scroll up to the top," Tracey instructs.

I scroll up to the article headline and read it in disbelief:

Brent-Sigma Pharmaceuticals Boss and Seth BioTech Founder Seen Out Together On a Date. Are the Rumors True?

My heart threatens to stop in my chest. I feel heat crawl in waves up my arms, to the back of my neck, up through the skin of my scalp to the top of my head.

This can't be, I think to myself. *Why would he lie?* I don't know whether I am feeling angry or sad, or both. Even worse, I don't know who I'm angry at. Myself, I decide. I had let this complete stranger in, and I gave him parts of me that no one gets. It is my fault that he lied to me. My fault that I was starting to have feelings for him. I'm the one who is stupid enough to get swept away in a fun game of excitement, desire, butterflies, hope, and distraction -- now duplicity, deceit, and lies.

I get up from my seat in the lab, knees shaky but somehow holding me standing. "Tracey, I just need a moment. Transfer my calls, no one sees me. No one else in the lab. I just need a moment." As these last words trail off, Tracey's eyes reveal she understands my meaning. She nods and motions me toward my office.

Is Ellis even his fucking name?! I close my office door and take a seat at my desk. Brent-Sigma is the pharmaceutical giant that is trying to buy its way into my company. *And he's the CEO?!*

I try to make sense of what makes no sense to me. What was he trying to get from all of it? Was he trying to get me to sell my company?

Shame washes all over me. I was such an easy target. So easy to get into bed. This feeling paves the way for rage, as I realize then that I am both crying and holding my hands in fists. I bang both fists on my desk and let out a guttural, "FUCK!"

Pull yourself together and stop being such a fucking crybaby, Alexandra. Self-fucking hard love. But yes. I know I must gather my senses and quit feeling sorry for myself. *I got myself into this shit*, I can't waste any more time not getting out of it.

Opening my fists and laying my hands flat on my desk, I close my eyes and take ten slow, deep, measured breaths. Holding in momentarily at the top, before fully exhaling with a low hum.

I open my eyes and calmly state, "I am Alexandra Seth. I'm badass. I am powerful. Strong. No one messes with me and gets away with it." I reach over to open the lower desk drawer and grab two tissues. Closing the drawer, I use the tissues to dab at the tears near my eyes and down my face.

It takes several minutes for me to feel adequately composed, or at least composed enough, to walk out of my office and talk to Tracey.

"Who else knows about this?" I ask her.

She waits for a second before she answers, no doubt because my eyes are puffy from crying, and she likely heard the loud F-bomb through my closed door.

"Everyone."

Chapter One

Ellis

Monday, Two Days Earlier

Within the past hour, my Executive Board and I had just finished discussing the plan to buy 30% of Seth BioTech's shares. In the last decade, it's been our mode of operating at Brent-Sigma Pharmaceuticals. Buy up smaller drug companies bit by bit. Then once we have the majority, break the little guys up into unrecognizable pieces.

So, this morning, when I walk into the coffee shop, I know exactly who she is.

Alexandra Seth: Founder and CTO of Seth BioTech.

Why haven't I seen her here before? A huge part of me is curious. I know the Seth BioTech offices are only a couple of blocks from here, but I have yet to run into her before today.

And I've stopped in for a coffee every day for the past month. This morning, she is standing before me.

Since my company is trying to buy hers out, there are so many reasons why I should turn around and walk away. My Board and the SEC being the top two reasons. It goes without saying that if I absolutely *have to have* my coffee, I should keep my eyes straight ahead while I'm standing in line, and I definitely shouldn't say anything to her.

But it. Is. Too. Hard.

With all the pros and cons I'm throwing around in my head, all of a sudden I find myself standing behind her. As she moves, I can smell her shampoo. Raspberries and flowers. How can I resist, as I breathe in short, greedy whiffs? I look around to see whether anyone else notices.

Don't speak to her. Don't say a word. OK, I've got this. All I need to do is keep my mouth shut.

"You should see a chiropractor about that." The words involuntarily slip between my lips, because I see her hand rubbing her neck. *What the actual hell?* But I can't help myself, I want her to turn to me. Hear her speak. To look into her eyes.

I can do a little homework for the company. Talk with her, share a coffee, get to know what she's thinking. But, who am I kidding? It's well-known in the industry that Alexandra Seth stays on the science side of things.

Two years ago, she hired a CEO to lead the business side of things so that she could focus her energies in the lab. I know that any digging I might do regarding upcoming research will just lead me down a rabbit hole. There's no way she would divulge her own company's secrets.

Funny, dude, how you're trying to convince yourself that this is a reconnaissance mission for company secrets. Hilarious, because she's the one attacking my good decision-making skills. Not even with stealth. I feel like it's all out in the open for everyone to see.

Shut up, dude. Let it go, Ellis. Why am I trying to engage her? But then she turns around and the reason is all too clear. I was a goner the moment I decided to walk into the coffee shop.

"Thank you, but I'll be fine." She responds. Her grey eyes are a striking contrast with her black hair, which she's wearing in a ponytail. Her hair is cascading down in waves and when she turns, the scent of berries and flowers invades my space, acting like a signature that she can use to mark me as hers.

When she lifts her eyes to meet mine and finally notices me, I can no longer listen to any voice of reason I might still have.

I am looking for anything that might convince me to leave this alone and bury it deep inside.

"I'll have what the lady is having," I say to the barista, letting out a small cough.

Alexandra Seth is dressed in khakis and a white shirt. I'm guessing that she wears a lab coat all day, so there's no reason she needs to be dressed in office attire. Her casual clothing doesn't hide her curves and my throat goes dry making it impossible to speak clearly. "Same, please," I confirm with the barista, to make sure I was understood.

I haven't been able to take my gaze off her, even though she looks away. Captivated. Intrigued. Mesmerized. Whatever the right word is for what she's doing to me, it's all the above.

"Are you sure? It would be a shame to see you having to make a doctor's appointment for something that could be so easily fixed." *Can I be any more boring?* I have zero moves. She makes me nervous and I'm struggling to think ahead to what I'm supposed to say to her. After all, she's the smartest person in this room.

"And you know this because you're a doctor?" She asks.

This makes me smile, but the universe would not be so kind to me as to make me an intelligent doctor. Someone worthy of her and up to her intellectual level.

The barista hands me my coffee. I nod in thanks, then look at Alexandra and say, "Well, not exactly, but I am familiar with the human anatomy." *What the hell?*

"Ah, let me guess," she starts to say as she takes a sip from her coffee, her grey eyes peering back at me over the lid of her cup. "You learned anatomy from all the women you take home every day. Perhaps from this very coffee shop?"

Her response gives me a chuckle, but then I start to laugh. She's quick-witted and one step ahead of me. Obviously, she knows that I have a reputation for dating a lot of women and not committing to any one of them. *Shit, she must think I'm disgusting.* I rack my brain for something that might save me and keep her talking with me.

"My mom was a physical therapist," I say. "I picked up a few tricks from her. So, I guess in a way, you are right. I did learn from a woman, but she took me home."

"I'm sorry," she says with a laugh. "But really, I'll be fine."

What am I supposed to say next? Dammit. I'm a bumbling idiot. I think about different topics that I can bring up to try to get her to stay and talk to me. Should I talk about my company? Should we talk about hers? Oh, hey my company is trying to buy yours out. There really is nothing I can say to her that will keep her in this coffee shop with me.

"I really should get going," she tells me. We've been walking towards the exit since we got our coffees and when she pushes the coffee shop door open, we turn our attention outside. We can see that there's now a sudden and heavy downpour of rain that God, some heavenly being, or the universe has sent for me. Whoever or whatever gave me this gift, I am eternally grateful.

"Let's wait it out together," I tell her, shrugging my shoulders while I look around. I spot a couple of stools at a bar-height table in the corner of the coffee shop and start moving toward them. When I get halfway to the table, I turn around and see that she's still standing by the door. I spread my arms out and say, "Okay, now I'm convinced you are just trying to get rid of me."

She peers back outside and for a moment I can see that she's debating whether to brave the weather or take up my offer. I feel a huge *fuck, yeah* when she starts walking over to me.

Offering my elbow for her to grab, I introduce myself. "I'm Ellis." *What is this, medieval times? She doesn't need my assistance to walk five feet to a table!* And as I'm kicking myself in my mind, she reaches out for a handshake. I unfold my elbow and offer my hand instead to return her handshake, very bummed that I didn't get to hold her hand close to my body in the crook of my arm.

As we sit down, she tells me her name, "Alexandra."

She wouldn't remain here, smiling at me, if she knew that I am Ellis Brent, the new CEO of Brent-Sigma Pharmaceuticals. Maybe she'll turn out to be a sour, grating bitch so that it will justify the plans my company has for hers. It is not lost on me that she didn't have a negative response when I gave her my first name. *Maybe she hasn't made the connection yet.*

"So, aside from being knowledgeable of human anatomy, what is it that you do?" she asks with a playful smile.

My heart jumps at this question. "Straight shooter, I like that," I say, with a grin, having to think quickly on my feet.

"Well, I was in the Marines for quite some time, but I finished my duty and I've recently just come back to help out with the family business." *Tell her that your company is trying to buy out hers.* I know that I should tell her the truth. Then I can get into why it's a good idea. But, then I'd have to tell her what my Board intends to do after we buy shares of Seth BioTech. Somehow, I think she must already know.

For now, I'll feel this out and just offer minimal details. Just in case she's the one trying to pull one over on me.

"Oh," she replies as she appears to be looking me over. "Thank you for your service. When did you get back?"

"Last month," I respond.

"Not taking any breaks I see." She assesses. Her eyes are hard to read.

I wonder, Is she digging for information by starting with small talk, or is she actually interested in what I have to say?

"How are you settling in? That's quite a transition you have going on," she asks, setting one elbow on the table and leaning in.

I try not to take that as a sign that she wants to know the answer. It wouldn't be a good idea for me to get ahead of myself. I answer, "I've never been afraid to make mistakes. I've also learned from mine."

The storm outside reminds us of why we're sitting together in this coffee shop. A powerful gust of wind slams heavy sheets of water against the window, causing several people in the shop to let out a combined gasp followed by muted remarks, most likely about the weather.

"But enough about me, what about you? What do you have going on that is really messing up your back?" I want to learn more about her, but I also want to direct the attention away from me.

"I'm a scientist." From her answer, it is evident that it's the science that she holds in utmost esteem. When she answers my question, her eyes light up like I have never seen in someone before.

She isn't offering the complete truth. It's true that she is a scientist. But, she's *the* Scientist. *She* founded Seth BioTech.

Alexandra *is* Seth BioTech. Seth BioTech *is* Alexandra Seth.

"Smart. I knew it. But, those Petri dishes can be hell on the lower back." *There I go, trying to pull off dumb jokes again. Back on track, Ellis. Back on track.* "What kind of scientist?" I ask her.

"I'm in biotech." She answers while seemingly searching my eyes. For what, I don't know.

When I was researching her earlier this morning, I was impressed by what she's been able to do for cancer research and immunotherapy. Having her in front of me, I really do want to ask her a thousand questions. But I'm nervous. "That's amazing. So, you study ways to help humans live longer and healthier." I'm genuinely impressed. "I had no idea I was in the presence of such an important person."

It looks like I've embarrassed her. She humbly states, "I haven't really done much."

"Even if that is true, and I highly doubt it, I'm sure you'll do something important that helps the world on a global scale. And soon." I'm in awe that she could be the reason for such incredible innovation and be so modest.

"How do you know?" Her eyes are still searching mine.

"I just do," I say without thought.

I can see from her expression that my remark has caused her to pause. I'm not exactly sure why, but I hope I haven't said anything to scare her off. "I just mean that I can tell from your face that you love what you do. If anyone can discover amazing things in the biotech field, it will be someone with as much passion for it as you obviously have."

After I say this, it does look like she relaxes a bit. But then she looks away from me to check the weather outside. *She is looking for a reason to leave.*

"It's just a light rain now," she notes to herself, aloud. Alexandra rises from her chair, and I stand as well, taking one more whiff of her scent, which sends a bolt of lightning traveling through my spine. But instead of enjoying what she's doing to me, I have to think.

I'm scrambling to figure out what I can do to get her to stay with me longer. I check my cup to see if there is any coffee left, but I have finished mine. And by the looks of it, she has finished hers too. *What can I do? What else can I talk about to make her stay?*

I clumsily blurt out, "I want to see you again."

When I opened the door to the coffee shop and first saw her, I was telling myself to turn around and walk away. But, I didn't. Instead, I've been sitting with her for the past half hour getting to know her. Really coming to like her. Wanting to spend more time together.

I gather my bearings and hope that I appear confident. I don't want to accept no for an answer. "Tonight." *What the hell are you doing, Ellis?* I question myself.

She parts her lips to speak, and I'm hopeful that she's going to say yes. But it's apparent to me that she's indecisive. I can tell that I've surprised her. Frankly, I am surprised at my directness. *She has to say yes to me. I want to see her again.* So, I place my hand over hers, and tell her, "Don't say no."

She knocks my socks off when she smiles and asks, "You don't give up, do you?"

It's not a 'no', so that's a good sign, I think. "One of the many benefits of being in the military. Just one drink. At Notre Terre. After that, if you want to bury yourself in work, I won't stop you. Maybe I'll even get you to fix that back of yours."

When she looks up at me, she seems to be searching my eyes again. It makes me wonder if she's asking herself the same exact question as I am. *What the hell are you doing, Alexandra?*

"Alright, one drink. Eight o'clock." She decides.

Chapter Two

Alexandra

Wednesday

*E*veryone. Tracey's answer is ringing in my ears. *Everyone* knows about me and Ellis.

After several seconds of just standing there trying to process the bombardment of thoughts and worrying about their implications, I begin calculating my next move.

Trying to compose myself, I smooth any stray hairs from my ponytail and ask her, "How do I look? Do I look OK?"

I ignore Tracey's piteous look that tells me *You should really look in a mirror.* She lies to me and nods, saying, "You look fine Alexandra."

Ugh!! Everyone's lying to me! And, don't fucking pity me. I shoot her an angry glare and turn on my heel to step into the restroom.

Luckily, I keep eye drops in the laboratory bathroom. After all, I have spent many late nights and early mornings in the lab. Getting rid of red eyes is a necessity before last-minute meetings. I place a couple of drops in each of my eyes and think about how I am going to get control of the situation.

First, I need to talk to my CEO, Lance, and clear up what the news means. Or, more importantly, what it doesn't mean.

I exit the laboratory bathroom, step over to the elevators, and press the Up button. When the doors open I press the button to take the elevator up to the CEO's office on the top floor.

Another woman is already in the elevator. She gives me a look like she is judging me, so it's fortunate for her that we share the elevator car for just two floors before the doors open and she steps off. I was on the verge of telling her she was fired, for eyeing me strangely. That would not be a good look for me.

When she gets off the elevator, two men are about to get on. But I step forward to block their way and say, "Take the next one." They know who I am and have a look in their eyes that shows they've made the connection between me and the headlines. The doors close as I see one man's mouth start to open.

While I'm riding alone in the elevator, I think back to Monday. This whole mess started on Monday.

As usual, I woke up at 5:00 a.m. and opened my email messages while drinking my morning coffee. It was then that I found out about the potential buyout.

With coffee in hand, I read through the message about the deal that my top executives had brokered behind my back.

Subject: Seth   BioTech/Brent-Sigma Pharmaceuticals Deal ... general meeting of all executive level associates ... discussion about the Brent-Sigma deal ... thirty percent of shares ... six hundred million ...

I was immediately angered by this news since I knew what the implications of such a buyout would mean. The big drug companies try to swallow smaller drug companies and market their products as their own.

In the case of Seth BioTech, Brent-Sigma just wants to shut us down. The therapies and treatments that we develop, effectively do away with the drugs that they sell. They're just looking for a way to kill my research or hijack it and milk it for more money -- and then kill it.

But, I have a promise to fulfill; to my mother, my grandmother, and to myself. They're the reason I started my company in the first place. Both my mother and my grandmother were in their late thirties when they died from breast cancer. I wasn't born yet when my grandmother died. But I was a young girl when I found out my mother had cancer.

I watched my mom go through rounds of radiation and chemotherapy. She fought with all she could to be there for her family. She endured so much suffering from cancer, its treatment, and the drugs she was prescribed, and it hurt immensely to experience it all with her, especially when we knew she wasn't going to make it in the end. When my mom died, I was 17 and I had already decided to devote my life to figuring out if there is a better way to treat cancer, and without drug dependency.

Later, Monday morning, when I arrived at my lab, I had the wherewithal to think about backing up important research onto an external hard drive. There were many things I was thinking about that gave me reason to want to perform this backup.

First, I knew that the contract I signed when I took the company public made sure that all of my antibody drugs and nucleic acid therapies that were already on the market, as well as all novel immunotherapy research and discoveries that were in the pipeline, would follow me if I were to leave the company for any reason. If there was a deal that my Board pushed through without my support, then I should make sure I am ready to leave with everything I have created.

Second, I had a feeling that I should be ready for anything. I didn't have any evidence that there was a threat to my research, but with everything that was going on behind my back, I just had a feeling that I should cover my bases.

After backing up the necessary information, I went up to the top floor to talk with Lance.

I hired Lance two years ago as my Chief Executive Officer, after taking the company public. Since my focus has always been on the science and technology side of things, I knew that I needed someone incredible to handle the business side. The shelves in his office boast the numerous awards and accolades that he's achieved: Salesman of the Year, Top Executive, Diamond Club, President's Status, etc.

So far, Lance and I have co-existed perfectly together. I moved into the position of Chief Technology Officer and other than the quarterly executive meeting, I haven't had to take my focus from the treatments and therapies we're developing.

But I went to Lance's office prior to the executive meeting in order to address the potential deal with Brent-Sigma. From day one, I have made it perfectly clear that big pharmaceutical companies' interests don't align with our mission. Period. There is no way we can ever let them buy us out. That's Lance's job. That's why I made him CEO.

I remember that there was something in his eyes. Something that told me he thought me standing there in front of him or what I was saying was all just entertainment.

Lance thought that I needed to be reminded that there were six hundred million dollars at stake and that there was a reason why I put him in charge of running the business.

I reminded him that he promised me something like this would never happen. He knew that I could take my research anywhere. I *would* take my research elsewhere.

So, when we went into the executive meeting, I made sure to remind everyone that I had asked them to give me a year to get our current project into clinical trials. Instead, just five months later they went behind my back to make this deal with Brent-Sigma.

In addition to letting the executives know that I could leave the company and take all my research with me, I firmly stated that Seth BioTech would never be affiliated with Brent-Sigma.

After the executive meeting, I felt that I successfully quashed the Brent-Sigma deal. However, I needed to get out of the building. So I went outside for a walk and decided to head to the coffee shop that is just a couple of blocks from the office. I've passed by it every day on the way to and from work, but I'd never been there.

I started thinking about how the Brent-Sigma deal had gotten as far as it had. It was because I was so focused on my research that I was looking the other way when my executive board made plans behind my back.

Brent-Sigma is the largest pharmaceutical company in the country, they're an old dinosaur. One would have to do some deep digging to find the last time they created their own drug. Nowadays all they do is buy smaller drug companies and put their drugs in Brent-Sigma packaging. But, their pockets are deep and I could see how my Board could have been lured.

On the way to the coffee shop, I made it a point to never again let my focus on the research take my eyes completely off everything else going on at Seth BioTech.

The coffee shop is where I first met Ellis.

I don't remember which came first: his low voice vibrating through my bones from his place in line behind me or his signature sandalwood scent.

***

The elevator dings, announcing I am almost at the top floor. When the doors slide open, I walk straight to Lance's office without talking with anyone else. The secretary eyes me heading for his office and starts to stand up. She says something, raising her hand to stop me.

"He's in?" I ask, as she nods and tries to speak. I raise my open palm to her and interject, "Hold his calls," I order as I enter Lance's office and close the door behind me.

"What am I reading here, Alexandra?" he asks. "Are you hiding something from all of us? I hope this photograph wasn't Photoshopped."

It isn't a surprise that Lance wants there to be ties between me and Brent-Sigma. So, it's important to set the story straight before ideas about what the news and photographs mean can spread in his imagination.

"Unfortunately, those pictures are real," I answer. As the words of my explanation start forming in my mind, I realize how truly humiliating and crushing the truth is.

"And before you plan a huge celebration, it's not what you're hoping for either. I still have no intention to cooperate with Brent-Sigma or to sell company shares." Good start, but I still need more time to figure out the whole story of what I want to say. What I need to say needs to be heard by the entire Executive Board.

Instead of continuing with the details of my side of the story, I order, "Gather everyone you can to the board room in fifteen minutes."

Incredulously, he states, "That's not a lot of time."

"Well, it's all I'm giving you," I answer back. "Make it happen."

I take a seat on one of the plush leather sofas, tilting my head and raising my eyebrows to inform him that I will be waiting there in his office until the meeting starts.

Lance stands up from his desk and walks out of his office, no doubt to talk with his secretary who will organize the meeting. I know that he could have just picked up the phone on his desk and made the arrangements. However, I have no doubt he wants to say things he doesn't want me to hear.

While waiting for the meeting to begin, I use the time in Lance's office to skim through the photographs and articles that are causing my current difficulties. I pull out my phone, open the Internet app, and type my name in the Search bar.

Usually, when you type in my name and search for me on the Internet, the Wiki page about me comes up first, then the Seth BioTech website, followed by hundreds of industry articles about my research, the treatments and therapies that have already saved or prolonged millions of lives, and similar articles.

Instead, I feel like I am hit by a boulder to my gut when I see that the usual search results are replaced with today's gossip pages.

Sorry Ladies, This Decade's Most Eligible Bachelor is Taken

Seth BioTech and Brent-Sigma in Bed Together?

Alexandra Seth: Sold Out, but Won Big

Brent-Sigma Pharmaceuticals Boss and Seth BioTech Founder Seen Out Together On a Date. Are the Rumors True?

The list of articles flow down to the bottom of the entire first page and although I don't click Next to see if they continue on to the second page or beyond, I figure that they do. And, they'd all contain the same type of information.

I scroll back up to the top of the Search page and click on the first article.

Sorry Ladies, This Decade's Most Eligible Bachelor is Taken

Freshly seated CEO, Ellis Brent, was spotted this evening with Alexandra Seth, the founder of leading Biotechnology company, Seth BioTech. The two were spotted holding hands and with heads together, apparently laughing at each other jokes. Perhaps this is a new age for Seth and her cutting-edge biotech firm.

I click back and open the second article.

Seth BioTech and Brent-Sigma in Bed Together?

It's a Cinderella story for Alexandra Seth as she appears to have captured the heart of Pharma's newly-crowned King, Ellis Brent. After the couple was spotted at a coffee shop together and later at the posh Notre Terre, rumors started whirling. However, talks between the two heads of Seth BioTech (Alexandra Seth) and Brent-Sigma Pharmaceuticals (Ellis Brent) weren't a surprising occurrence.

The couple's status was confirmed with photographs of Ellis Brent leaving Seth's home in the early morning hours before the sun even came up. Brent and Seth were photographed later in the day having lunch at an out-of-the-way diner and then at the movies. Sources close to the couple confirm their connection and say they're taking it one day at a time.

Does this mean that Brent-Sigma will be the parent company of Seth BioTech? Or, will Brent-Sigma merge Seth BioTech into the fold to create an even bigger Pharma powerhouse?

The titles of all the articles in my search turn out to be versions of the same gossip. So, I don't read anymore. It is all just as I feared. *Well planned*, I think to myself. Ellis has had it all figured out from the start. *And to think I—*

The door opens and Lance peeks inside the door of his office. "We're all assembled in the conference room and waiting for you." I get up from my seat and follow Lance into the conference room where I see that all the same players from the previous morning's executive meeting are again assembled to hear my explanation.

"I assume that by now you have all seen pictures and articles that tie me and Ellis Brent together," I announce when I place myself at the head of the boardroom table. Anyone who had risen from their seat when I entered the room has returned to their chair.

"I'm assuming you have an explanation," one of them bites back, almost immediately. "You sat in that very seat and said you wanted to end every issue concerning Brent-Sigma. And it turns out…"

"It turns out that there still remains no business connection between Brent-Sigma and Seth BioTech." I cut him off before he has a chance to finish. "It's a ruse, but not a very clever one." I don't want to give them a chance to ask me why I was at the movies with the CEO of Brent-Sigma, so I just keep talking.

"This morning, in the lab, we verified the results from the research of our latest immunotherapy treatment and are excited to inform you all that our findings are a success. We are ready to move into the clinical trials stage." After saying this, I can see a new sense of satisfaction cross the faces of most of the partners and executives.

With this news, they know that there will be a surge in company confidence, and with that confidence, there would be a rise in stock prices and interest in further investment. "I have already instructed my assistant to get that ball rolling. All departments should be receiving this information as I speak."

"So, I'm not going to waste your time and mine justifying what you see and what you will read in the headlines. These are just tabloid stories. I hope that with our own research moving on in the development stage, you'll remember that I continue to fulfill my promises to you." I look around the table and feel accomplished to see that they are all sitting quietly, interested. "I hope you'll remind yourself of that fact. Just in case you ever again think that we should sell shares to any Big Pharma company."

"I'll end what I need to say with this: My stance remains the same. I have never intended, and I still do not intend to let

Brent-Sigma buy into my company. There is not now, nor will there ever be, any cooperation between us. Their interests do not align with our mission."

It dawns on me that I had never taken a seat, so I don't have to rise from a chair. "That's all there is for now. Thank you all for attending this meeting. Have a good day." I turn on my heel and walk out the conference room door.

On my way to the elevator, my phone buzzes, and I tap the screen to see who it is. Instantly, I feel a fresh wave of rage to see Ellis's name.

Although I decline his call, I do want to know if he was telling me the truth or lying. *Who am I kidding?* I reason. Of course, he was lying.

In the elevator, I stare at the *Missed Call* on my phone screen. I don't want to hear his voice. All I'll get is more lies.

Not. Any. More.

Chapter Three

Ellis

Tuesday

I stir from my slumber, one eye starting to open, and I see that the sun still hasn't come up. Looking at my smartwatch, it's 5:34 a.m. I feel a wave of calm satisfaction take over when I see her face in front of me and she's still asleep in peaceful slumber.

Slowly, I try with everything I am not to move the bed. I don't want to wake her. But, as soon as I have one foot out from under the covers and off the bed, her eyes flutter and I see I haven't succeeded.

"Hey beautiful," I tell her in a hushed whisper. "Good morning." I pull my leg back in bed and roll over to give her a kiss on her temple as berries, flowers, and her soft, smooth skin threaten to hold me hostage in her bed.

"Good morning," she replies as I force myself out of bed and reach for my clothes. As I'm dressing, she looks at her phone, likely checking the time and wondering why I'm leaving so soon.

Hoping that she won't get the wrong idea, I make sure to tell her, "Last night was…"

"…amazing." She has stolen the words right from out of my mouth.

She has taken hold of me and all I want is to stay here in her bed with her and never leave. I want this. I want her. I want to see her again. There are so many thoughts racing through my mind right now, but guilt invades my conscience, and I can't run from the fact that I could be the reason that she loses everything she's worked so hard for her whole professional life.

When I leave Alexandra's house, I can't shake the feeling that she knows who I am. *How could she not know who I am?* I remind myself that there's no way she would give me the time of day if she knew. But I am sure that, all too soon, she will find out.

At some point, probably when she gets back to her office, she is inevitably going to encounter the truth. I need to get to my Board members right away in order to convince them to release the hold they are so desperately trying to get on Seth BioTech.

She can't find out that I'm Ellis Brent of Brent-Sigma Pharmaceuticals before I can completely shut down the threat that my company has over buying part of her company. She will never forgive me for lying to her.

This needs to be fixed now.

First I drive home so that I can change before heading into the office and am overwhelmed with the flood of thoughts drowning my brain.

While I'm definitely thinking about Alexandra and the night we just shared, I can't help but remember my parents and the family business that has been thrust into my responsibility.

Brent-Sigma Pharmaceuticals is the largest pharmaceutical company in the U.S. My great-grandfather, Louis Brent, founded Brent Pharmaceuticals in 1934. At the time, we were one of the leading innovators in our field, developing life-prolonging and life-saving drugs that people have depended on to this day.

My grandfather became the President in 1958 and Brent Pharmaceuticals became Brent-Sigma Pharmaceuticals when it went public in 1960. By the time my dad took over as CEO in 1987, Brent-Sigma had risen to international prominence in the pharmaceuticals field and to #1 in the U.S.

When my dad took over, we had just started changing our business model from focusing on drug development to swallowing up smaller companies and getting bigger. Even though most of our products nowadays are just Brent-Sigma packaging slapped onto one of our subsidiary's drugs, Brent-Sigma is heavily built on the trust people have in my family name. To this day, we are still the largest pharmaceutical company in the U.S.

I begin thinking back to yesterday, Monday, when I left the coffee shop after meeting Alexandra.

It was puzzling to me why she didn't seem to know who I was. Just four months ago in July, my parents died together in a car crash. It was all over the news and you have to have been hiding underneath a rock to not have heard about it. When the crash happened, I was abroad, in the Marines, about to re-enlist for another four years.

All my life, I have been groomed to take over the top spot, but none of us ever expected me to take over so soon. My dad had been CEO for 26 years when he died. He was in top shape, and it was easy to believe that his health would have let him lead for another 26 years or more.

So, when my mom and dad died, it was a surprise for everyone at Brent-Sigma. When given the choice to become CEO or re-enlist, it was an evident decision for me and when I finally completed my job in the Marines, I moved back home last month and became CEO of Brent-Sigma Pharmaceuticals.

Meeting Alexandra at the coffee shop yesterday was invigorating. There was a pep in my step, and I felt great. Except, I knew what I had to do. I had to figure out how to go back to my Board and direct them away from Seth BioTech.

As I was walking back to the office, all I could think about was my date with Alexandra later that evening at Notre Terre. *Shoot, I should have offered to pick her up.*

I called my secretary and asked her to find Alexandra's cell phone number and text it to me. Less than ten minutes later, I got the text and dialed the number right away.

"Hello?" Alexandra answered. As soon as I heard her voice, I hoped that she didn't think I was a creeper and was stalking her or something. She didn't give me her number, so I got that it could appear strange that I was calling her after parting ways less than twenty minutes before.

"Hi Alexandra, it's Ellis. I was getting back to my office and I'm sorry that I didn't even ask you if you wanted me to pick you up for our date." If I just kept talking, maybe she wouldn't think to ask me how I got her number. "Can I pick you up and we can go to Notre Terre together?"

"No, but that's really thoughtful. I don't live far from the restaurant, so I'd rather just drive myself." She had already planned her evening, so I decided not to push it. "Plus, it's only drinks," she added.

No! I want it to be more than just a drink. Thinking about how to convince her to stay for dinner, I thought about pulling out some charm. "I don't know if you've been to Notre Terre before, but it's one of the select Michelin-star restaurants in the area. I'd really enjoy your company over having to eat alone tonight. Will you stay for more than drinks and have dinner with me?"

Yes! Her answer is yes! I tried to hold back and not sound overly excited, but when our call ended I pumped my arm back and exclaimed, "Oorah!"

When I returned to my desk after meeting Alexandra at the coffee shop, all I had to do was tap the space bar on my keyboard to show the Seth BioTech website. Alexandra's face was peering back at me, since it was what I was browsing before I left the office to get coffee.

... Alexandra Seth, four-time award winning Biotechnologist of the Year ... saves more than half of a city poisoned by chemical waste ... is she the future of modern medicine?

... Seth BioTech making waves across Europe, Africa, Asia ... threatens to rival some of the greatest there ever was with her unique techniques ... and that face! ... Who knows if and when she's going to consider marriage. Sources have been unable to confirm the presence of a man in her life ...

I was already beginning to think I couldn't go through with the Seth Biotech deal after meeting Alexandra Seth. Reading articles about her, I became sure that I didn't want to keep trying.

However, I knew that the deal was exactly what my Board wanted, and I had no doubt many on the Board were just waiting for me to fuck up. And when I did, I'm sure they'd waste no time taking the company from under me.

But, I couldn't let that happen. I imagined that my dad would turn over in his grave. My father always wanted me to take over the reins at Brent-Sigma and I can only feel sadness that he died before he could see it.

I had only been in my office for a short time when Richard Cross barged in, impatient to talk to me.

There is no stopping people like Richard Cross, one of the family business' first investors. There has never been a time in my life when Richard wasn't around. He's basically family. I stood up and walked over to embrace him in a hug.

"I'm sorry I couldn't make it to the funeral, I was tied up in Croatia. It's a shame what happened to them." I had poured two glasses of bourbon for us and Richard took a sip from his glass. "I heard the first attempt to buy out Seth BioTech didn't go so well. Understandable though, because of your parents' passing."

"Yes," I answered. I couldn't help to think that he could care less about my parents' death and only how the circumstances would affect his earnings. But instead of confronting Richard and accusing him, I saw it as an opportunity to bring up what I was thinking about ever since I got back from the coffee shop.

"Maybe we should venture elsewhere, Richard. Or better still, come up with something innovative of our own." Richard stared back at me for a few seconds, like he had seen a ghost. I was sure that he was going to say something that would make my skin crawl. Instead, he burst out laughing, hysterically, like I had just cracked the funniest joke in the history of running a business empire.

Richard's laugh was spine-tingling and eerie in its ability to explain that he saw nothing funny about what I had just said. "You know how it is in our line of work," he finally said, after finishing his wave of laughter. "It's a dog-eat-dog world out here. The reason Brent-Sigma is as big as it is today is that your father made sure he was the biggest and baddest dog of them all. He was always the first to buy out small startups. If they didn't comply, he always found complex ways to tear them apart."

I knew that he was talking about lines that my father was willing to cross in order for Brent-Sigma to continue to grow into the global prominence it is today. Richard is not only talking about lines that needed to be crossed but also new lines that needed to be drawn – the lines that he and my father had crossed and drawn together.

"I'm sure you'll figure it out, son. It's like being in the Marines. You may not know it yet because the numbers haven't started to drop yet, but mark my words. We are at war." His next words were slow and calculated. "Seth BioTech is the enemy."

When Richard left my office yesterday, the last words he left me with were, "Remember, Ellis, we are at war." His words still hung in the air even after I was the only one in the room.

***

I'm still thinking about yesterday's run-in with Richard and the night I just shared with Alexandra when I arrive at the office just before 8:00 a.m. I'm surprised to find Richard, and another Board member, Bart, already in the office and standing outside my door.

"Ellis, great," Richard says, appearing excited to see me. "I was just going to call you. I…we have an idea about how to cripple Seth BioTech. You will come to really like it—"

"About that," I interject, to his apparent disapproval. "I was thinking we should take our eyes off Seth BioTech."

Richard steps back, with a look of concern on his face. Yesterday, when I told him, "Maybe we should venture elsewhere" or "come up with something innovative of our own," he burst out laughing. Today, he's not laughing, and this time he seems very irritated.

"What are you talking about?" Bart asks. Since he has to ask this question, I can tell that the conversation I shared with Richard yesterday had no bearing on him. He just brushed my ideas aside and didn't feel the need to talk about them with anyone else.

"This again? I thought we buried this discussion, son." When Richard makes this remark, it confirms that I should be concerned that was his takeaway from yesterday's conversation.

After the talk Richard and I had in my office, I thought that there was a possibility of taking Seth BioTech off the table. At least something to explore. But now, hearing Richard basically saying it was never on the table I knew I needed to speak to the entire Board.

If Seth BioTech is to be kept safe from my company, I need to be convincingly clear that I don't want to go after it again and I need to provide an alternative solution that the board members will go for.

"Call a board meeting," I command, not allowing anyone to sway me this time. "I want everybody in the board room in ten minutes."

Fifteen minutes later, I am sitting in the CEO's chair with eight pairs of unsatisfied eyes staring back at me. The air is hushed and so tense you could cut it with a knife.

"I'm sure you all know why I called this meeting," I start, knowing that Richard and Bart have prefaced the meeting for everyone with their own opinions.

"Let me be absolutely clear." And as I look around to make sure everyone is listening to me and there can be no cause for misunderstanding, I say, "We are letting the Seth BioTech deal go."

Sixteen eyeballs display looks of dismay, disbelief, bewilderment, surprise, and especially doubt. Every single one of these people are looking back at me with doubt over whether I'm the right person to be sitting in the CEO's chair.

After about a minute they all start to murmur and bicker amongst themselves.

One board member, a woman with tightly bound, red hair, speaks up first and says, "You must not know everything there is to know about this deal and why it's necessary that we move fast. They're going to become a problem if we don't sink them now. They've already cut six percent of our consumer base with their latest therapy. With every new thing that comes out of there, we know what comes next. The gradual, then speedy decrease in our profits."

She continues speaking, "Brent-Sigma is a titan in our industry. We've come up in the pharmaceutical world by being the biggest bully in the yard. It's why we are so dominant and why we are so feared. Our competitors know how we handle every weed that sprouts in our yard. We uproot them. If Seth BioTech, or any other weed is allowed to invade our yard, or worse, if our competitors fund these weeds themselves, together they could run us down."

I attempt to assure everyone that couldn't happen and that Seth BioTech has no plans of merging or selling a majority of its shares to any other company. But then an assertive voice booms from across the room.

"Not unless we give them a reason to." Richard shoots me a cold glare as he conveys a controlled anger that would be enough to scare most people.

"What if it does happen?" A different woman, named Belinda, asks. She has dyed, curly, blonde hair. "What if they sell shares to any of our competitors?" Belinda's voice is flat and sharp. I have always had the feeling that she is the most dangerous one in the room.

"They won't." I couldn't see how Alexandra would sell to anyone, not after she has been offered a whopping six hundred million dollars for just thirty percent.

"And you know that how?" Belinda asks.

"I have a source," I add. "We already offered six hundred million. Are we going to offer a billion? Two billion? They're not going to take it, even if we sign that we're not going to discontinue their research."

"So, what? You're just going to give up? Your father would have found a way." It's clear why Richard has made this statement in front of everyone. Not only do I think that he's trying to get on my nerves, but he's likely also trying to get me to do something that will give them reason to strip me of my position as CEO. Make it easy for them. But I am not going to let him.

"I'm not my father," I tell him, looking around at everyone to emphasize this statement.

"Clearly," Richard huffs. He sits back in his chair, crosses his arms at his elbows, then looks away.

The tension in the air tightens again and it's several seconds before someone else speaks.

"You're putting us in a real tough spot here," a ruddy-skinned board member says. "We have been running things like this smoothly for over 70 years. No hiccups. We were bringing in profits. We still are. But letting that company grow from underneath us…that's just—"

It's been eighty-nine years since my great-grandfather founded Brent Pharmaceuticals and sixty-three years since we went public, but I don't correct him. "Crazy? Irresponsible?" I offer up these words for him instead. "That's what you all brazenly have written on your faces. But I can remember a time when all this wasn't just for the money. There was a time when all of this had meaning." I throw my hand, palm up, and wave it across the room above everyone's head, to signify the entire building.

"We haven't developed a new drug in five years. How long can this business model survive for a pharmaceutical company in these new times? All we're interested in now is raking in profit. I've got to say, I'm disappointed." The whole room falls quiet, thinking.

I'm relieved to notice that some of them know the truth about what I am saying. However, the board members with the most influence, like Richard and Belinda — the people who cross, erase, and draw new lines — they barely seem affected by what I am saying.

"You're right, Richard. I'm not my father." He peers at me, his eyes glaring. I continue, "So don't expect me to do things exactly the way he did."

The side of Richard's mouth curves, almost to a grimace, before settling into a cold smile. Similar to the laugh he showered me with yesterday when I told him that I wanted to look at companies other than Seth Biotech, his smile hints at a sly calculation of something yet to come.

But that is something I will have to deal with later.

Richard stands and says, "You are more like your father than you think." He then walks out of the room.

Richard's exit draws an exclamation mark in the air above everyone remaining at the table. Finally, the red-haired woman inquires, "What do you want us to do now?"

"Go back to the drawing board," I tell everyone. "It's the twenty-first century. Let's lead the way so that others will want to follow. Let's figure out new ways to save the world. Because whether it's Seth BioTech today or some other new, innovative start-up company like them. It will be them, not us, who are going to lead the way into tomorrow. Then, we will truly be in a tough spot."

"Let's figure out what we need to do to be leaders in the twenty-first century." I look around at the seven pairs of eyes left in the room and see what I hope is a glimmer of understanding. "We're leaving Seth BioTech alone."

When everyone leaves the room, I think about yesterday's conversation with Richard and what just happened in the board room. A huge sigh escapes me, and I know that my main worry is with Richard. I am certain that manipulating lines to get what he wants costs him nothing.

There is a different feeling in the office after I leave the conference room. A kind of tension that can't necessarily be explained, but shows up in things like people looking up at me but then either immediately looking away or doing things like pretending to remember something they forgot and then turning to walk the other way. No doubt, word has spread about my decision not to follow up with Seth BioTech.

I wonder, *Does everyone think I am inexperienced, foolish, a coward, or just idiotic?* But, I know that there's not enough time in the world to waste on things I can't control, namely what others think of me.

While I know that I need to eventually find Richard and get him to understand why we shouldn't go after Alexandra's company, first I need some air. I need to get away from this office and see if I can clear my mind of any self-doubt before I can address any doubt that others might have about me.

I head back to my office to inform my secretary that she should push out all my meetings until the late afternoon.

"Can I borrow this please?" I ask as I grab a random book from her desk without first inspecting it. "Just going out for some air and a quick read. I'll bring it right back." It isn't my intention to read the book. It's just a prop to appear busy.

She opens her mouth and raises her hand to say something, but before my secretary can protest, I rush out of the office. I get in my car and drive to a small mom-and-pop place that I know of, where no one knows that I am the CEO of a multibillion-dollar empire.

It's a place I know well from my high school years as being a simple diner on an out-of-the-way strip of road leading to a stretch of highway that is sparingly dotted with little farming towns.

"What can I get ya?" The waitress asks me with a smile. She recognizes me from the many times I have come here, but not from the news or tabloids. I've been coming here since I got my driver's license and was able to drive anywhere I wanted.

Just as I'm about to request a waffle and a cup of coffee, I spot Alexandra sitting on the far side of the diner, staring out the window, into space.

I order coffee and motion toward the other side of the restaurant, "I'll be swapping booths." The waitress glances over in Alexandra's direction, then back at me, understanding my intention.

"Coming right up," she confirms while she's walking away.

I slide out of my booth, grabbing my book. Excitement fills my bones with each step I take toward Alexandra. When I left her this morning, I was already looking forward to figuring out when the next time would be when I would get to see her. And here she is. She's sitting in the same diner as me.

"Now I'm convinced you're following me," I say as I scoot into her booth, sitting opposite her.

This booth has the least lighting, and the restrooms are on the opposite end of the restaurant. Other patrons won't be walking in this direction unless they are also seated here near the end. I can see why she has chosen this spot out of all the seats in the diner.

Clever. She doesn't want to be seen. I like how she is so aware of her surroundings. I find that it's such an attractive quality for someone who is independent and can think for themselves. *She's here to get away, just like me.*

She looks away from me like she isn't happy to see me after our night together. Scanning the diner, her eyes eventually circle back to me. I think she must be coming to terms with the fact that I'm not leaving.

"How did you know it was me?" She inquires, like her disguise is wasted. She is doing that thing again where she looks into my eyes and is searching for something.

"Wearing a baseball cap and sunglasses indoors is a surefire sign you're trying to hide, and therefore some people would be more likely to check you out to see if you're famous. It does the opposite of what you're trying to accomplish. Plus," I tease, "It's hard to walk into a room and not notice you. Maybe, it's impossible." A smile sneaks across her gorgeous face. *And there she goes again. Pulling me in like a tractor beam.*

"Listen, if this is about last night—" she starts to say, pulling her shades down from off her face.

"It's not," I begin to say, even though if I am being honest with myself, it is a little bit about last night.

Having her here in front of me, I know that I have wanted to see her again since I left her in bed this morning. If I didn't have to make sure her company was safe from mine, I would have stayed with her all day and left only when she asked me to. Maybe never, if it were my choice.

I look across the table and see that there is only a cup of coffee in front of her. "What are you doing here? You don't look like the pancakes and sausage type." I am certain she hasn't touched her coffee.

"I like to come here sometimes. To clear my head," she explains after a few seconds, "This is somewhere where I never bump into someone I know."

"I get it. Believe me, I do." After her last statement, it still seems like she doesn't know who I am. "I did some digging on you, Ms. Seth. I had no idea you were such an important person." Lie.

"Don't worry," I reassure her. "Your secret is safe with me."

To my surprise, she says, "I know."

She gestures to the book in front of me and asks, "What are you reading?"

The waitress arrives and drops a cup of coffee before me, with a smile on her face. "Need anything else?" I tell her we're good for now, then she leaves after I give her a grateful smile.

I look down at my secretary's book that I borrowed as I was heading out of the office. I didn't even look at the cover when I took it since I didn't have any intention of actually reading it. A book can be a useful prop to look like you're busy so others don't think they can bother you.

While Alexandra tilts her head and tries to make out what is on my book, a perplexed look suddenly appears, and she reaches across the table to turn the book over. She pulls the book towards her to get a better look and reads the title, with surprise.

"Billion Dollar Baby Daddy: An Enemies to Lovers, Secret Baby, Off-Limits Romance," she reads aloud, each word in the title sounding more ridiculous than the last. She breaks into hysterics, trying to hold it together so that she doesn't cause a scene.

Should I be embarrassed about what she might think about the string of red flags I've been presented to her over the past 24 hours? First, I call her with the number that she didn't give to me. Then, like a stalker, I show up at this out-of-the-way diner at the same time she's here. And now, I have given her a reason to question my free-time reading preferences.

But, I am enjoying watching her laugh so freely, as if the world isn't on her shoulders. So, I join in on the punchline. "True life romance fiction is my jam," I announce with confidence. "This is the sequel to Billion Dollar Baby Mama Drama, which was itself just a literary phenom."

She takes a second to think about my last statement and when she's sure that I'm only joking with her, she laughs uncontrollably, which I also find makes her damn sexy.

When her laughter is calmed to small giggles, I ask her, "How?" She looks at me, trying to figure out what I'm alluding to, and I clarify my question.

"How do you know I'm not just going to scream that the founder of the leading company in Biotechnology is here? The woman who has saved countless lives?" I am just joking with her, but I am also curious. Alexandra's face starts to flush with pink and she shoots me a gaze that reads, *You wouldn't.* I shake my head to infer that *I won't.*

She searches my eyes again. "You're not the type," she concludes, sure of her answer. I feel honored to receive her confidence in me.

"Go on," nudging, and wanting her to continue.

"It's just…yesterday at the coffee shop, you said I was going to do amazing things with my work, and you also said you just knew. You're the loyal type. I can tell." She's sincere as she's telling me this and I'm secretly hoping that loyalty is a quality that she holds in high esteem and that she sees it in me.

I do think of myself as a loyal person. A loyal Marine. A loyal American. Loyal to the values of what our American flag represents. A loyal son. I could also be a loyal friend.

My heart does belly flops in my chest, and I feel like laying myself prone before her and telling her everything she should know about me. The truth, all of it.

I start thinking, Isn't there a right time for the truth? Or, if everything goes as planned and I'm able to redirect my Board's interests to different sights, there's a way that who I am doesn't matter and the timing of when she finds out won't matter.

"You don't know me." As these words escape my lips, I think Dammit. What am I doing? Am I trying to stir up the hornet's nest?

"I feel like I do," she confidently reveals. "Ever since last night ..." I watch her eyes veer off as her confidence fails her and her words trail off to a different path. "Though a part of me wonders if maybe you don't want to see me again. I met you only yesterday and everything was so instant and fast. I was so easy. You left."

As I let her finish everything she has to say, my heart bursts with joy as she exposes how my actions affect her. Not because I've made her question my intentions, but because what she's telling me shows she cares.

My eyes seek hers so that she can see just how sincere I am when I tell her, "I had a wonderful night with you. The best night. And I couldn't wait to give you a call later today. But obviously the universe has other plans for us." My hands and face gesture to the diner and the booth we're sitting in, hopefully explaining that *since we're both here by coincidence, there's a higher power that wanted to get us back together*. "My mind never left you this morning, and I've been thinking about when I get to see you again."

Her grey eyes look into mine, either digging for something to believe in or for something to doubt. "What are you doing here? Really."

"I don't remember how long it's been, but for years I've come to this diner to just get away from everyone. Not that I've had an awful life, but from the first time I came here I felt like it was MY place. I can come here and just spend all day reading, alone." I pick up my secretary's book and pretend to be nose deep in reading the story about the billionaire baby daddy. Alexandra giggles and my heart does flips.

"Last night at the restaurant, I was telling you a little bit about growing up in El Dorado Hills. I said it was a great place to grow up, and it was. My friends and I were given the freedom to ride our bikes anywhere we wanted around town. And we'd go to the lake all the time, just to jump in and hang out there all day. Life was good, I really can't complain." Thinking about before I started high school, I feel so nostalgic and wistful for those carefree times.

"Around the time I started high school, my dad started to bring me around the office more to let me sit in on meetings and business deals. Grooming me to be the next in line to head the company." While I talk, I notice that I'm unintentionally shuffling the book back and forth between my hands. So I slide it back to lying in front of me, remove my hands from the book, and clasp them in front of me on the table.

"I have always been interested in the family business and I also can't really complain that my teen years were split between hanging out with my friends and learning how to run an international company. My life was privileged and easy, compared to most. Anyway, when I started driving, I would just choose a direction and drive. Just to get away from the expectations and pressures I felt at home. And, that's how I found this place." I point up and look around the diner.

"Since I got out of the Marines, I have found it's still my very own place of peace." When I say this, she nods, and I feel like she gets me. Understanding that indefinable something that this diner has that keeps me coming back is something that she and I have in common.

"I completely know what you're saying when you describe this place." Her shoulders, once high and tense, ease a little and

I watch as she smiles more. It makes me feel happy knowing that she's relaxing around me and worrying less about anyone recognizing her. "Sounds like taking over the family business is proving to be quite a challenge." She hits the nail on the head, and I feel a little tension myself as I am reminded of what's going on at work.

"It has its moments," I tell her. "Some of the people who should have my back, because of family ties and long-standing friendships, don't agree with my ideals and it's causing a lot of friction."

"Oh, that," she agrees, "That I completely understand." She looks at me and I can tell that she's thinking that she's told me more than she wanted. I know from all the reading I've been doing about her and her work that she hasn't been telling me half of who she is or what she does for a living. But I'm not going to press her about it. After all, I'm not telling her much about me either. I don't know the reason, but she's not asking.

Then I start thinking about whether she's known this whole time who I am. *Is she just pretending not to know so that she can get information from me? What if I'm the one being played here?* But I feel like I know her. Like I can trust that even though she's not telling me everything about herself, I still know that she's not trying to pull one over on me.

"Ellis," she says, calling me back to the present. "Are you all right? I was saying how I was going through something similar at work."

"Oh," I shake my head back and forth as my heart skips a beat. I clear my throat and sit upright in the bench seat to gather my bearings. Either this is a test, or she really doesn't know who I am. "How so?" I ask.

She looks straight at me, apparently figuring out if she can trust me, and she releases a deep sigh.

Dude, this is the perfect time to come clean. My guilt is burrowing deeper and deeper into the pits of everything I do, everything I think about. She's going to find out sooner than later. It's better coming from you.

Finally, she leans forward, as if she doesn't want anyone else to hear. "There's this company…they're trying to buy a stake in mine," she confides. "But I know they're just trying to shelf my research."

"What you do is important work, Alexandra," wholly believing what I'm saying. "No one should be allowed to do that."

"I know," she says. "I'm doing everything in my power to make sure this deal doesn't happen."

"So don't sell," I tell her as if it is as simple as that. I can imagine a cartoon image of Richard in my mind. He is holding a box with TNT written on it over his head, which then explodes. *Tell her now that the company she's talking about is yours. This whole thing will explode if you don't tell her now!*

"I'm not," she says. "That's not entirely the issue." I feel like she's looking at me and searching my eyes for something, though I'm not sure what. "You know what? I don't want to put all my problems on you. Let's talk about something else. What is it that you do anyway? Your company."

I had prepared something to say, knowing that she would eventually ask me this very question. But my entire body hesitates for a moment, scrambling to organize what I am supposed to say. I can't stop thinking, *just tell her the truth.*

She's about to say something because I've taken a bit too long to answer her. But I rush to tell her the lines I've been rehearsing. "A lot of what we do has to do with real estate investments and other endeavors."

As soon as these words come out of my mouth, I kind of hate myself. I've sort of told the truth. Since last year it's true that we did purchase all the land needed to expand one of our major facilities. We also bought two other plots of land, but they so happened to have small drug companies on top of them. So, all in all, still lies. *Ugh, I'm such an idiot.*

"Not nearly as interesting as what you do." I tack on. So ready to have the topic changed.

I'm relieved when she asks me if I like animals and have any pets. It's so easy to be around her. It helps me temporarily forget the pressure I'm putting on myself to have to tell her the truth now, at this very moment.

Talking with Alexandra is fun and easy. She has such an appreciation for life and helping others and it shows in what she likes to talk about. I can't help but fall for her when I see how she lights up as she shares how she enjoys the work that she does. And what her vision is for helping those with various diseases live longer and pain-free lives -- free from the dependence on drugs.

The more time we spend together, the more I know that I don't want to leave. I don't know if I'll ever be ready to leave. And I can tell when she smiles at me that she doesn't want to leave either.

Chapter Four

Alexandra

Tuesday

After running into him at the diner, Ellis and I have decided to keep our date going and catch a movie. So, I'm back at my place to get ready and I have until 4:45 p.m. when he's picking me up.

While I'm getting ready, I dreamily recall the events of the past 24 hours. Starting with the coffee shop, then our date last night at Notre Terre. *Oh my, I've only known him for 24 hours. I've never felt this excited about anyone like this before!*

While I want to remember every last detail about our date at Notre Terre, much of it is lost in a blur. Probably because I was nervous. Maybe because I felt so much excitement about the possibility that I already felt in our new connection. I had just met Ellis, but what he made me feel (what he makes me feel) was intense and I'd already developed a tower of expectations and hope for what there might be between us.

When I arrived at the restaurant, the amber-gold lighting that surrounded the building acted like a backdrop to my dream-like state. Notre Terre is one of just a handful of Michelin Star restaurants in Sacramento, but I had never been there before. I expected something elegant and it did not disappoint.

As soon as I walked into where Ellis was waiting for me, I felt his eyes hot on mine, trailing down my curves to the slit on my dress. It was a look from him that I had been craving since we first met. It was the reason why I picked that red dress out. I noticed the longing in his eyes and reveled in the fact that he appreciated the dress on me and wanted it off me.

Ellis had reserved an entire room in the restaurant for just the two of us. A lone table was arranged in the center of the room and when I walked in, Ellis stood up from his seat.

The saying that "he took my breath away", is 100% true in this case. I breathed in and then out. When I saw him I am pretty sure that I had to take in two breaths because there was barely enough oxygen in the room to prevent me from passing out. He was impossibly even more handsome than that morning.

Wearing a grey suit without a tie, he had left the top button of his shirt unbuttoned. I didn't doubt that we were undressing one another, not caring that the restaurant staff was in the room with us.

Over the next hour, we shared the most amazing meal I've ever eaten, I laughed harder than I have ever laughed, and the sexual tension between us quite possibly could have blown the roof off the place.

I was surprised at my ability to maintain my composure, because I remember that it took all my strength to not crawl across the table, pull that man by the collar, and suck his tongue right out of his mouth.

When we were finished with dinner and it was time to leave, I tried to perform a body scan to determine how much wine I drank, and what my level of sobriety was. I wondered how I could make sure this night wasn't over. *Am I holding myself up, or is Ellis the only one keeping me steady?*

My body scan informed me that I wasn't drunk, just happily buzzed. But he said that he'd drive me home and have my car brought to me by the morning.

He drove me to my home on Winding Creek Road in the Arden Oaks area. His sandalwood scent was all over his car, sending my nerves firing. As we were walking up to my front door, my mind was racing. I kept thinking that I didn't want the night to end. *He's giving me signs like he feels the same things I am. What should I do to make sure this night continues?*

I turned around to face him when we got to my door. My eyes investigated his, trying to hold them and find the signs I was searching for. The ones that could help guide us to whatever would happen next.

"Good night, Alexandra. Our date is the best I've ever had. I had an incredible time meeting you today." He waited for my response. *Is this pause a sign? Does it mean he's hoping I'll reach up to kiss him? Do I just ask him to stay?*

It surprised even me when my lips parted and I asked him, "Well, are you joining me inside?"

He instantly rewarded me with his smile and a hunger in his eyes. My senses were firing, and I was a sphere of exploding fireworks. At any moment, I could lose control of my actions. If I hadn't lost them already. My body took control, and I reached out my hand to him. He took it, following me through the door.

The front door shut behind us and he moved behind me, bending down and burying his face in my neck. *Lock the door.*

Grab a glass of water. Do you need to go to the bathroom first? Is my room clean? The rational part of my mind, the part that is normally in control, was trying to be a source of reason.

But, when I felt his hot breath on me as his mouth brushed my skin, my pulse quickened, and I uncontrollably released a weak moan. My knees buckled and threatened to collapse under me. He pulled me in close, still behind me, and I felt his bulge on my butt through my dress.

Fuck it. Just give in. A stream of electricity and chaos traveled through my spine as soon as his hands cupped my waist. His face was burrowed into my shoulder, near my neck. I reached my hand up to grasp his hair, guiding his head to continue its journey.

He kissed my shoulder and opened his lips to lightly suck my skin, seeming to mark a starting point. His tongue then traced up my neck to the bottom of my earlobe, leaving behind a wet, merciless trail. He lifted his mouth from my skin, seeming to pull my body with him. Not wanting his mouth to stop.

But, then he blew a focused breath along the trail his tongue had just paved, searing my senses. Inching me closer to my point of no control.

His mouth returned to my neck and then his tongue expertly flicked my lobe as he exhaled hot breath into my ear, the depths of my desire listening. Aroused, but also impatient, I felt an urgency within. I turned around to offer him my open mouth, hoping that his own would satisfy mine. My body was begging, and his lips appeased mine as turmoil was arising within me.

Everything felt perfect; it was all perfect. I accepted his offering, greedily, twisting my tongue with his. Feeding a hunger that had been building in me since the moment we met. He lifted me up when I wrapped my legs around his waist and the slit on my dress ripped further. The low, drumming hunger that had invaded every part of my body that he now touched, was increasing in rhythm and intensity. One of my arms grabbed around his broad shoulders, securing him to me. My other hand held his head as he pressed warm kisses on my neck, down to my collarbone. Then he started walking forward, up to my bedroom. Knowing right where to go, as if he had been in my home before.

When he stepped into my bedroom, he eased me onto my bed, our lips now locked. I willingly submitted as our tongues slid around one another as if in a ravenous battle. Somehow, and I wasn't completely sure how, he managed to get my clothes off. He slid my dress and undergarments up, down, or around from off my body. When they were off, all I wanted was to feel his skin on mine.

My hands desperately worked on the clasp of his belt as he took off his shirt. Within seconds, I pulled his bulge out and felt a wave of pleasure as it pulsated in my palm. Ellis kicked off any remnants of his clothing and came down on top of me, pressing the weight of his entire body on mine.

Aching for his touch, my grateful body surrendered to him. His skin next to mine, the weight of him reigning in the sparks of pleasure that were surely and madly radiating from my core, barely contained within our sphere. His tongue, again finding my lobe, anchored to my ear as he whispered, "I want all of you, now."

"Oh Ellis, yes." I could barely breathe out my consent because he pressed another passionate kiss onto my mouth as he slid inside me. The moans escaping me were choreographed only with the oscillations and undulations of our movements, and he rewarded me in return with groans originating from deep within him. We were unhesitating and sure in our actions, as if we had done this together hundreds of times before. I clawed my hands into his lower back as we rocked together, back and forth, sending waves of pleasure firing through me with every thrust.

He flipped me and changed our movements to his every whim, seeking my gratification and I was showing him how to find it. I was close when his tongue was exploring between my legs, and I pulled him up to join me. "I want you inside." And helped him travel upwards to obey my request.

All I wanted was to feel his whole body yield to me, and when I started to feel the inevitable climb to my own apex, his pleasure was synchronized with mine. Up and over my peak, fireworks and explosions went off and my body was tensing and releasing, pulling him deeper within me, I felt him arriving at his point of no return.

"Say my name." I groaned into his ear.

And while he released within me, he surrendered to me. Gasping, "Alexandra."

***

My smartwatch reads 4:30 p.m. and I realize that I've been daydreaming about last night with Ellis. *I hope tonight is a repeat*, I think to myself.

I don't have much time until Ellis arrives to pick me up for our movie date. So I shake off the deliciousness of feeling hot and bothered and I change into jeans, a pale yellow, V-neck tissue tee, and brown platform loafers.

I'm just finishing up a retouch of my mascara when Ellis's text pops up on my phone letting me know that he's outside waiting for me. I grab a lightweight, white, cropped jacket from my closet on my way out the door, and I meet Ellis next to his car in my driveway.

He makes my heart skip a beat when I see him. He's wearing an A's baseball hat, a white, short-sleeved Henley, and white court shoes. Seeing him casually dressed in clothes that he wears every day outside of work has me wanting to get to know him better. There's so much more I want to learn about what he enjoys doing and who he is.

He takes me to the movie theatres at the Palladio outdoor mall in Folsom. It's a popular spot and even though there are hundreds of people, we have more fun than I expected. He's thrown on a brown leather jacket and we blend in with all the other movie-goers in the theatre lobby.

We're so engrossed in the fun we're having that we don't think twice about who might see us. It feels to me like no one can possibly know who I am. No one cares. I'm just another woman out on a date with a gorgeous man.

It's packed inside and outside the theatre because it's the big blockbuster opening night for <u>Star Avengers VI: Night on Planet Zero</u>, starring Ben Watts, and the theatre is packed. Every movie that Ben Watts touches is a hit and I know that the entire crowd is here to watch his movie. I look over at Ellis and notice that he's in his own world, chuckling.

It's then that he shows me what he thinks is so funny. Our tickets aren't for the <u>Star Avengers</u> sequel, it's for a rom-com starring Jessica Strait and hunky Brock Nolan. I suppose I didn't care much about seeing the <u>Star Avengers VI</u> movie, after all I think I just saw the first one and possibly parts of the next four movies in the series. I am a bit surprised though that Ellis wouldn't want to see it. I thought all guys liked action movies.

Ellis jokingly tells me, "You already know I'm a secret fan of steamy romance, so I got these tickets in hopes that I can pull you over to my camp."

"Oh, I get it," I reply. "You want to suffocate me with cheesy romance plots until I can't take it anymore and I agree to do whatever you want."

"Wait," he says with a silly grin on his face. "That's a possibility? Yes! I knew I had the perfect plan!" He pulls me close and plants a kiss on my head, as we navigate away from the crowds and into the theatre where our movie is playing.

"Good call by the way," I whisper over to him when we're finally in our seats. "Oh, I have to put my cell phone on Silent." I pull out my phone to flip it into Silent mode.

"Which call? I'm constantly making so many of them," Ellis says as he also puts his phone on Silent mode. "I want to make sure to take credit for the right one."

"On choosing this movie to watch on the first day that Ben Watts's new movie is released." I look around at the empty theatre, "We have our own private showing."

"Ah, ha ha ha ha," he cackles, tenting his fingers and squinting his eyes, "Yes my dearie, all part of my plan." His devilish grin is irresistible, and I love how we can so easily joke around and let loose around one another.

The movie opens with Jessica Strait driving a car through the lush wine country. She is speaking in a voice-over of the scenes, like we're in her thoughts. Jessica Strait's character is named Mya and she arrives at a multimillion-dollar vineyard estate for the combined bachelor and bachelorette parties for her best friend, Victoria, and her younger brother, Case. Jessica Strait's character is smart, sassy, and drop-dead gorgeous.

The scene changes to Brock Nolan swimming in the pool on the estate. He is known for his incredibly muscled and tanned body and is the perfect actor to play the leading role in any romantic movie. In another voice-over, we find out that he plays the role of Liam, a troubled ex-military turned mountain man.

"This plot seems to be right up your alley." I look around and see that we're still the only ones in the theatre. I tell him my version of the movie's plot, "Headstrong city girl meets military/survivalist ... together they persevere six nights in the unforgiving wild and relentless weather of the California wine country."

He lets out an appreciative chuckle, then says, "Our story is my favorite." He nears his face towards me and teases my neck and ear with his breath. "What do you think?" he whispers.

"Hmmmmm. I definitely like how it's going so far." I turn my face to him and brush my lips across his. He leans towards me, but I pull back playfully, saying, "Peppy and ambitious salesgirl meets cutthroat and grumpy billionaire... he propositions her to act as his fake fiance to save her from a mountain of debt, but it's she who actually saves him." I giggle as I move towards him and plant a kiss, parting my lips, pressing my tongue forward, hoping to play with his.

He seems to pause for a moment and I temporarily insert doubt in my mind. But I decide I am mistaken when he returns my kiss, satisfying what my tongue is seeking. It's driving me crazy that he's weaving his fingers through my hair, pulling my hair slightly.

"I want to feel you." He breathes into my ear and I move closer to him as his mouth continues to cover mine.

He moves a hand under my shirt and the entire front of my stomach feels small, covered in whole by his large palm, which he then moves around my back, then up my side. He is causing me to moan uncontrollably. My sounds and the way I move when he touches me is turning him on.

He reaches up to the top of my bra and pulls down the lace to tease and lightly circle my nipple with his finger. I feel the urge to jump on top of him as he covers his large palm over my breast.

His tongue and his mouth feed off the pleasure within me. For him, I have a constant supply and he'll just find more.

As he moves his hand down to the button of my jeans, I think *These damn jeans*. I have no interest in this movie and

I'm convincing myself that it doesn't matter that we're in public, I want to have him again. *We're alone.* Persuaded by my desire, I move to jump into his lap.

"Shhhhhh!" Comes from somewhere within the theatre, along with some unintelligible whispering. I'm jarred back into the here and now and I reluctantly slink back into my seat.

I look over toward the direction of the speakers as they come up the walkway into the theatre. Another couple has entered, and they walk up the aisle stairs to find their seats. We're no longer alone.

There are bits and pieces of the movie that I'm catching and I can tell it's a comedy as well as romantic. But being this close to him and not getting to touch or be touched by him is driving me absolutely insane. I'm having a hard time enjoying the movie because for the remainder of it, all I can think about is what I want to do with Ellis when I get home. What I want him to do with me. Definitely a repeat of last night.

So when the lights come on and we stand up to leave, I am a ball of pent-up energy and I can't stop talking. All the way home, I joke about the movie and come up with ridiculous romance plots for romantic comedy books and movies that I can tease Ellis about.

When Ellis pulls up to the curb in front of my house, I tell him, "Come here handsome," and I grab his chin and pull his face towards mine. It should be very clear to him that I don't want this night to end here. We're going to continue what we were starting to do in the theatre. "Stay with me again tonight?" I barely get this question out between hungry kisses.

His lips are telling me *yes* and he confirms their meaning by saying, "I want all of you." He steps out of his car and circles around to open my car door.

I do another body scan. *Clean, lacy underwear. Sexy bra. Maybe a quick trip to the bathroom. Ooh, maybe some toys?* I am feeling impatient, thinking about having his body next to mine. Being with him.

I look in the passenger sideview mirror and don't see Ellis walking over to open my door for me. Spinning my head around I see that he's stopped by his trunk. So, I open my door and stick my head out just enough to peek back and ask him, "Is Everything OK? That long trip around your car is taking you too long. I'm impatient, but luckily I know how to open my own car door." I swing my legs out of the car and Ellis walks up, reaching his hand out to me.

We walk to my front door and I'm desperate with desire. On my front porch, I spin around to face him and playfully ask, "So are we going to continue writing our story?"

He bends his neck down to return my kiss and my body instantly reacts to his touch. This man is everything I need in this moment. I breathe in his musky, sandalwood scent and I feel him swimming around in me, reaching and taking hold of my self-control. He is claiming me, and I will give him my whole body.

But as I'm willfully drowning in his rapture, his hands leave my head and waist and push at my shoulders to separate us. My lips on his the last I feel of him.

Ellis groans and tells me, "I can't stay tonight. I have to go."

I take one step away from him. Partially so that I can remain standing, as I do feel like falling backwards. But I also need to look in his eyes and make sure he's not playing with me. It feels like I've been slapped by a whoopie cushion to my face. That's a strange thought, but it's what crossed my mind because I'm stalled by the shock of it and at the same time, it has to be a joke.

My eyes, though, don't deceive me because I can tell in his expression that he is not playfully teasing me. He's not trying to get a rise out of me, only to pull me back in and do with me what he wants.

Pained, like a dagger has been thrust into my heart. And confused, because my body is still reeling from the passion it was feeling just moments earlier. I say, "Alright. Then, thank you for tonight," and I turn to walk inside.

Chapter Five

Ellis

Tuesday

It was one of the most difficult things I had ever done; leave Alexandra alone and drive away.

I panicked.

When I saw the headlines and message notifications flooding my phone, my instinct was to run. Get out of there fast, figure out what fires I needed to put out. Fix it before it destroys everything between us.

When the lights came on in the movie theatre, Alexandra threw the back of her hand to her forehead and made up a romance plot, saying, "Whew! so glad they ended up together with everything they had going against them. Just goes to show that if you can make it through a flying bottle of champagne and a full body cast, then you can make it through anything together!"

All the way to her house, Alexandra was having fun making jokes about the plot and making up new plots for cheesy romantic movies.

Meanwhile, I was stuck on what she said about making "it through anything together." My thoughts swam around, going over the possibility of whether Alexandra and I could also make it through whatever we're faced with. Together.

When I parked my car in front of her house, she pulled me into a dizzying kiss after I turned off the engine. She asked me to stay the night with her again and I could barely control myself. I felt crazed with yearning and hunger for her body against mine.

It's me and Alexandra again tonight. She is everything I want and I'll stay all night, I thought and knew that I just had to meet with my Board tomorrow and completely shut their plans down for good.

I stepped out of my car and while I was walking around to get to Alexandra's door, I remembered that I still had my phone on Silent. Part of me knew I should leave it be, but my mind was also drowning in guilt and self-loathing, so without thinking, I switched it back on.

Immediately, I heard a collection of dings alerting me to new headlines, messages, and calls. I glanced down at my phone and saw the first couple of lines of a News thread.

Seth BioTech and Brent-Sigma in Bed Together?

Seth BioTech CTO Alexan...

The passenger side car door opened and Alexandra peeked out, "Is everything OK? That long trip around your car is taking you too long. I'm impatient, but luckily I know how to open my own car door."

I helped her out of the car, and we walked up to her door. It seemed like the longest 15 yards I had ever walked because I was stuck in limbo between never wanting to leave this woman's side and knowing that there were fires that I needed to put out.

Alexandra spun around when we were facing each other on her front porch. "So are we going to continue writing our story?" She asked, reaching her face up. I instinctively bent my head down to kiss her. Her body reacted instantly as if switched on, and blood immediately rushed to my groin. She rubbed against me, and I grabbed her tightly around the waist, ready to lift her up, carry her into the house, and take her right inside the door.

Instead, my mind brought me back to the reality that Alexandra's company and mine were now tied together somehow in the latest headlines, and I needed to find out what that news was.

I unwillingly removed my lips from hers and groaned words that I didn't agree with, "I can't stay tonight. I have to go."

She stepped back, still looking up at me. Questioning me with her grey eyes that suddenly turned cold. "Alright. Then, thank you for tonight."

When she turned to walk into her house, I impulsively grabbed her by the hand and spun her back towards me. "The last thing I want is to leave, believe me. It's not my first choice. But tomorrow. I hope I get to see you again tomorrow."

Then I pulled her into my arms, into my firm hold, and filled my mouth with hers, taking in what I could.

Just in case it was the last time she'd let me.

***

When I leave Alexandra's house, I drive my car around the corner and out of sight so that I can stop and read through the first article. As soon as I do, I know that I have to address my executive board first and put an end to ideas that these headlines mean cooperation between Brent-Sigma and Seth BioTech. I have to make them know that there won't be a buyout, a merger, or relationship of any kind between our two companies.

Even though it is 10:45 p.m. at night, I immediately drive to the Brent-Sigma headquarters, then walk straight up to the board room and sit at the head of the table.

Alexandra, please pick up, I think as I thumb to Alexandra's contact information and tap her phone number. My heart drops to my seat when I see that it's going straight to voice mail.

I open the Messages app and text Alexandra. *I'm fixing this. Will call you soon to explain.* Send.

Next, I call Richard. After just one ring, he picks up with elation in his voice. "Ellis my boy! How's it going, son?"

Richard's happiness can only mean one thing. *Holy shit. He's seen the news.*

"Richard, I want to call an emergency board meeting. Fifteen, twenty minutes. Just a heads up." Short and succinct. He doesn't need to know any more details.

"Sure thing buddy! I'll wait for the link. See you soon!" He hangs up before I can. After that call, I know that I have to cut off the fires of misinformation before they spread.

I try to reach out to Alexandra again, but again it goes straight to voice mail.

Everything will be all right. Please call me when you can. I type into my messaging app. Send.

Next, I call my secretary, Cynthia. Three rings and she answers, "Hello?"

"Cynthia," I start, "Sorry it's so late. I'm in the boardroom right now. Can you please set up a video conference with all the board members? 11:30 ... so 15 minutes from now."

She confirms a few things with me before we get off the phone with each other.

While waiting for the meeting to start I glance through the articles about me and Alexandra. It seems that the number of articles has doubled since I saw the first one about an hour before. Every article tells the same story.

I'm the most eligible bachelor. Taken off the market by the princess of Biotech. Then varying reports of how my behemoth of a company must have plans to overtake her innovative, yet fledgling company.

I switch over to my email at 11:28 p.m. and click on the link to the board meeting. There are six members in the meeting already, but I hold off on niceties until the actual meeting starts.

At 11:30 p.m. on the dot, everyone has joined and I start the meeting. Beginning with my wanting everyone to know that the articles and photographs, although real, absolutely do not mean that I have changed my mind from the meeting we had earlier in the day.

I can tell from Richard's face that this is not what he expected to hear in this last-minute meeting. He wears the same face of disappointment and disbelief as I had seen on him earlier that day, now with a tinge of anger.

I echo the words from our last board meeting. "Let me be absolutely clear. We are still letting the Seth BioTech deal go."

No one interrupts me, since I muted everyone else for this meeting.

"But, first. I will provide you all with details regarding the sightings of me and Ms. Alexandra Seth." This is the information they have all been waiting for.

"I met Ms. Seth in person for the first time yesterday in the coffee shop down the street. It surprised me, but she did not know who I was."

I continue. "I recognized her the moment I saw her. She stood in front of me in line and I decided to talk with her because I was genuinely interested in meeting her. I didn't have any ulterior motives or intent to dig for company secrets."

"Over the course of the past two days, we have gotten to know one another. And that is all. Ms. Seth and I never once talked about a connection between our two companies." I can tell that I have all of the partners' attention now. "And that's all I need to say about that."

"So, redirecting to what is truly important, back to the subject of our company." Everyone is still apt to pay attention.

"Brent-Sigma's new direction is to go back to what made us big in the first place. Our innovation. The drugs that we developed that have since saved or prolonged millions of lives. So, in addition to continuing to add or merge companies into our fold who want to work with us, we are again going to create, modernize, and be the leaders in advancements in our field."

I pause for a moment to emphasize again this last important detail, "And, again, we're leaving Seth BioTech alone. Period."

After the board meeting, I see that the last two people still online are Richard and Belinda. When I click the button to leave the meeting, I immediately think, *They're up to something*. But if that's the case, I'll deal with them later. I sit back in my chair and know that I'm determined to figure out how to set things straight with Alexandra.

Chapter Six

Alexandra

Wednesday

This morning started off marvelously, with waking up hopeful about my relationship with Ellis and finding out my research is a success. Then it did a total nosedive and I felt like I was doing a walk of shame through my own company up to Lance's office and into this morning's board meeting.

For the rest of the day, though, I work with Lance and my executive team, and I manage to convince them to terminate the Brent-Sigma deal. Everyone is satisfied that our latest product is moving to the clinical trial stage, and we focus all of our time on that transition. No one talks about the tabloids. At least when they're in the room with me.

I get the feeling from the way a few of my board members still look at me that they are thinking that I am irresponsible. No doubt they have their own judgments of the news stories about Ellis and me. But, it's my choice what information to share and keep private, so I just have to brush aside those feelings I have about what others might think of me.

I'm thankful that the actual business of running my company has kept me occupied. Working with Lance and my Board is giving me more of an appreciation for what they do and why I hired them. It's another reminder why the Brent-Sigma deal threatened to sneak through. I can't be so entirely focused on the science and completely disregard the business side of things.

Throughout the day, I didn't have a lot of time to think about Ellis. And, when I did, I was quickly distracted by some important business detail.

It's after work now and I will thankfully wash away the stresses of the last ten hours with a warm shower, then relax with a bottle of wine.

The shower water travels over my body and it feels as if the water is washing away the heaviness I am feeling. I comb my fingers through my wet hair. Imagining that I am washing the events of the past three days off my body, out of my mind, and pushing them down the drain.

I find myself gritting my teeth while in the shower. I am contemplating what I am going to do to put out the slow-moving gossip fire that Ellis Brent has caused at my company and with the public.

Ellis has been calling, leaving voice messages, and texting me all day. He has left text after text asking me to let him explain and to give him a chance. *Give him a chance to tell me even more lies. Humphhh.*

He had two days to tell me who he was. OK, I get it. What he told me was the truth. But what he omitted was basically lying to me. No matter how you justify it, they were all lies. How could he?

The thought of being in the same space with him reignites the pain of knowing that our time together was all a lie. Shame is a cruel bully, stomping on the ashes of what I had hoped we might have been. It has also been harassing me because I was falling for him.

Even though I had managed to convince some of the board members that it was all a misunderstanding, a few of them had looked at me like I was irresponsible. It was hard to shake off the feeling of that embarrassment. It's still difficult to shake off that feeling.

I am also wondering what I am going to do to put out the fire that Ellis Brent started within me. It's been so long since I had been with someone. It was nice to have the fire fueled again. But really, he means nothing to me. Move on.

After my shower, I walk downstairs to my kitchen and open the wine refrigerator. *Feels like a Petite night.* I pull out a 2018 Petite Sirah, open the bottle, and take a grateful whiff of the cork.

Ellis isn't important. He's now in my past. I think to myself. However, I realize that even if I'm not ready to speak with him yet, I know I'll want to see him eventually. *Even if it's just to tear out his eyeballs and smash them into the concrete.*

I have just poured myself a hefty glass of wine when my phone, which is sitting on the kitchen counter, vibrates and plays a familiar ringtone. Without having to look, I know it is Tracey, my assistant. I also know something must be wrong for her to be calling me at 8:00 at night. My mind briefly sifts through some possibilities for what could be happening, but I don't delay in picking up my phone and answering.

"What's wrong?" I ask, cutting right to it. I take a sip of wine. The distant sound of a siren can be heard in the background. Tracey's voice is quivering, afraid.

"The lab … I did what I could … I'm sorry … fire everywhere." She takes gasps between her words. "It started out of nowhere. Everything's lost!"

"How did this happen? Are you alright? Is anyone hurt?" I ask. "There are special vents installed for this exact purpose. The sprinklers I had installed were supposed to be sensitive to even a matchstick."

"I don't know," she replies. "But you had better get over here as soon as you can."

"Are you alright?" I ask her again. I am hoping with everything in me that no one is hurt or worse. I hear a man in the background asking Tracey to take her statement. She tells me she is fine before she ends the call abruptly.

I stare at the freshly filled glass of wine on the kitchen counter. *Dammit. On a night that I needed you the most.* I grab a bit of plastic wrap, cover my wine glass, and recork the wine. This small action of preserving my glass of wine for later leaves me with a slight sense of satisfaction.

Before leaving, I change into a sweatshirt and sweatpants and grab my keys on the way out.

When I arrive at the Seth BioTech office building, there are two fire trucks parked outside, along with seven or eight other fire and police vehicles, and an ambulance. This vehicle causes me some alarm. *I hope no one is hurt.*

I park my car near the first responder who looks like he might be in charge. He is talking to someone on the phone and another person seems to be on some sort of tablet, providing him with information. Lance is also standing next to him, looking upset.

While I walk over to them, I look over at the Seth Biotech building to see if I can spot the damage. I can make out the part of the building that burned on the fifth floor. The lab. *Thankfully, the damage didn't spread more than that floor because of the safety measures that I had installed.* I look around to search for Tracey but get first to the man who appears to be in charge.

"Hello, I'm Alexandra Seth. This is my company." I reach my hand out to shake hands. He stretches his right hand out to me, so I clasp mine with his, feeling the coarseness of his palm.

"Hello Ms. Seth. I'm Captain Price with the Sacramento Fire Department." He shakes my hand and reads the look on my face.

"There are no deaths, and Mr. Tyson here has confirmed that all employees have been accounted for. If that's what you're worried about." He places one hand in his pocket and uses the other to point up to where the fire broke out. "Your assistant pulled the fire alarm as soon as she noticed the fire. Gave everyone a chance to evacuate the building."

While there are no injuries or casualties, my gut feeling is still telling me that something about this isn't right. To have a fire start in my fireproof lab the same day my research moves on to clinical trials and photographs of me and Ellis Brent surface online. I don't believe this is all a coincidence. Or an accident.

"Captain Price. Lance. Where is Tracey, my assistant?" I am still looking around for her but haven't yet located her.

Captain Price steps back and spreads his arm out towards one of the fire trucks. "She's right this way, Ms. Seth."

I walk with Captain Price around the fire truck and am relieved to see Tracey sitting beside it, covered with a warm blanket.

"Hey, are you hurt?" Instinctively, I lean over and give Tracey a hug. There is a hint of hesitation from her, but it is my guess that it's because we've never hugged before. We've been working closely in the lab for 4 years together and are with one another more than we're not. But we've never had a reason to hug.

Tracey tips the glasses on her nose and nods *yes*. As tears start to form in her eyes, I tell her, "I hear you're alright. To me, that's all that is important. I'm so relieved you're okay. You pulled the fire alarm, didn't you? It's because of you that no one else was injured, or worse!"

Poor Tracey seems to be in shock, I assess, as she is just able to sniffle and nod in response. "Don't worry about anything Tracey. You're safe and just take all the time here that you need. I'm just going to step over there with Captain Price to see if he has any details that he can tell me."

I walk over to Captain Price. "Excuse me Captain. Is there any information that you can provide me?"

His voice is gruff, and he has a bit of a Southern accent. "My men are still combing through, but it seems like it's just the fifth floor. Those fire hazard protocols you placed on the floor and ceiling of the entire lab made sure the fire didn't spread too far."

Another deep sigh of release escapes my lungs.

"But what I can preliminarily tell you is that the cause of this fire seems unnatural," he adds.

"How do you mean?" I inquire, not surprised.

"Well, I went through your fire protection system. Everything seemed to be intact and in working order. All systems were active on the fifth floor, except two. Both your carbon dioxide suppression system and your sprinkler system were turned off by someone on the inside. Someone tampered with your system Ms. Seth."

Just as I thought. And my suspicions first point to Brent-Sigma; Ellis Brent to be precise. And just as I was thinking about him, a text from him flashes on my phone screen.

"*I heard about the fire. Are you okay?*" I ignore the message and slide my phone into the pocket of my sweatpants.

"We already questioned your security guard. He said that he was out for a coffee break when the fire started. The second guard was home sick." I am lost in thought, trying to figure out exactly how Brent-Sigma is involved. However, it is the fact that they were able to carry this out at all that baffles me. They might have tried to make it look like an accident, but made some mistakes that hopefully will point right to them.

Another fireman steps up to Captain Price and taps his arm. The Captain leans his ear back and tilts his head while the fireman says something to him that I can't hear. Captain Price turns back to me and says, "If you need anything, please let us know. We will compile a comprehensive report of our findings and make it available to you as soon as possible. I've got to continue with this investigation now though, Ms. Seth."

Both firemen walk away, leaving me and Tracey. I turn to her. "Are you sure no one else got into the lab before the fire?"

"No," she answers. "That's not possible. I have been here since you left."

I lean closer to her. I don't want anyone else to hear what I am about to ask. "And our research?"

She looks around for a second before answering. "I was able to get two out of the three racks before the fire became too hot."

"How are they? Where are they now?" I ask, desperately. The last stage of testing depended on those three racks.

"They're still viable from what I could see. But we'll need a standard lab to test them. They're in the secondary lab."

"Good," I say with relief. The secondary lab is a smaller lab that only she and I know about. "We'll move the samples to my lab at home when everything settles down. Everything about this smells fishy."

"You think this was intentional?" She looks horrified. "Who would do such a thing?"

Without saying a word, I shoot her a glance that suggests: *you know who*. She opens her eyes, bright and beady.

Several minutes later, I hear the firemen confirm that the fire has been completely put out and the fire master confirms that he is right—my system was tampered with. He walks over to me to tell me he is sorry for my loss of property and heads out.

From out of nowhere, Lance sidles himself next to me. "Jesus" He mutters under his breath.

"Contact the insurance company," I say aloud. "I want this place back to standard by the end of the week. No one goes into the building until further notice."

"Already done." He answers quickly. If there is one thing about Lance that is true, he is always one step ahead.

Just then, the security guard who was on duty walks up to us, looking gloomy. He is a middle-aged man, with kind eyes that seem resistant to look into mine, like he figures he is about to be fired.

"What is it now?" I grunt. I don't know why I am being so gruff. I don't think this was his fault, after all. I look at his name tag to remind myself of his name and try my greeting again.

"Saul, I'm glad you're alright. Do you have anything you need from me?" I ask.

"There's somebody here to see you." Saul seems to relax a bit, but his eyes change to a look that says he is ready to get out of there.

"Who is it?" I ask. But Ellis steps out from around a truck and his appearance answers my question.

"It's me." The moment he comes into view, I feel a surge of rage come up within me. I move forward to him immediately, not completely sure what I plan to do when I reach him, but I have my fists balled up, ready to punch him in the face.

"You have the nerve!" Lance barks at Ellis as he grips my biceps with both hands to hold me back. "We're not trying to be charged on assault." He yells at me, as he moves to stand in front of me with his hands spread out, blocking my path.

"He did this!" I scream in Ellis' direction. "He's behind all of it.'

"Let's wait to assault him when we can prove it." Lance says. "Don't beat him up just yet."

"I promise you Alexandra that I had nothing to do with it." Ellis pleads, seeming sincere. A sliver of me wants to believe him. I want it to be possible that he had no idea about what went down. I mean, *how could you have that look on your face and still be guilty of something like this?*

Then I remember, Well, it's that same bullshit look that he's had the past couple days while he lied, time after time to my face.

"Yes, you fucking did!" I feel a maelstrom of emotions begging to be let out. "And when I find the proof, I'm going to rain a lawsuit against you and your company. You're going to wish you never met me or came after my company!"

Ellis is standing still. Sorrowful eyes are set on me. He doesn't say anything, and his look confuses me. *Obviously he is upset because he knows he's in a world of trouble. Not because he cares about what I think of him.* His choice to say nothing angers me further.

"You know what, Ellis. Get the hell out of here. I never want to see you ever again!" Yelling at him helps, since I can see my words have pained him. But there is still more I want to say; more I want to do. He should also suffer the feeling of loss that I am feeling. He should have everything that he cares about threatened to be taken from him.

"Fine," he surrenders, softly. "You can throw all the lawsuits you want at me. But just remember that *I'm* the one here. *I* showed up. And despite how my board members would hate that I'm here right now, *I'm* taking this risk to tell you I had no part in this."

"Then you're either ignorant or a master liar. And from my experience, it's the latter."

Being able to tell him these words gives me a strange sense of satisfaction and calm. Although, I don't like the fact that there is a part of me that wants to believe he is telling the truth when he denies anything to do with the fire.

I am firmly holding on to that part of me that is still hurt by his lies, from his smiles, because of the way he makes me feel. It's that same part of me that opened up to him. The part that allowed him to walk right in and trample on everything that I wanted him to have a piece of.

"Fine, I'll leave. But, not because I want to. You should know that I very much want to be here with you to tell you everything. To convince you that I'm telling you the truth." He is able to read my face and body language because next he says, "I will leave. Because you've asked me to. And because I'm going to get the proof that I had nothing to do with this fire." With that, he turns and leaves.

Ugh, I was such an easy target. Ashamed and livid, I just want to stand here alone with my thoughts. "Go," I say calmly to everyone.

It isn't until then that I notice that the security guard had already rushed out of there. Lance and Tracey look at me like they are assessing my sanity. I shoot them a cold glare and they turn around to leave.

When they are gone, I remain standing, looking toward the burned building. My thoughts focus back on Ellis, and my stomach twists into knots.

"I'm not done yet." He tells me. I turn my head, to view the face of the man I want to throttle.

Chapter Seven

Ellis

Wednesday

It is already a long day spent meeting with my board members and various upper-level executives. We've been discussing their part in figuring out how to start developing new drugs again and how to court the types of companies that want to work with us towards mutual advancement.

I am still at the office at 7:55 p.m. when I hear about the fire. I glance over at the television screen on the wall across from my desk, and see the headline scroll across the news ticker tape at the bottom of the screen. My heart immediately sinks. I grab the TV remote and change the channel until I find another news station that is actively reporting the story about the fire.

The reporter is standing in front of the burning office building. I turn up the volume.

"Witnesses say that the blaze spread quickly across the 5th floor of this West Sacramento building, which is occupied by the cutting-edge biotechnology firm Seth BioTech. Here I have Fire Captain Adam Price with me to give us a current update. Captain Price, what can you tell me so far about this fire and what it's taking to put it out?"

I look over at the glass door to my office, to what is now an empty hallway. Moments earlier, Richard and Belinda were standing within sight. *Can I draw a thin line from the news on the television to what Richard was whispering about? Was this what he meant when he said my father would have dealt with the issue? To be the bully of the corporate world?* I immediately stand, feeling heaviness. I don't want to believe that they are capable of endangering lives for the sake of profit. However, this kind of thinking is naïve, and I know it.

I look for the remote and turn up the volume even higher.

The fire captain is saying that the fire only hit the fifth floor. Targeting and incinerating everything in the laboratory. The guard who had been on duty stepped out for a ten-minute break when the fire started.

I am relieved to hear that there were no injuries or deaths reported. So, I know that Alexandra is alright. *But what could have started the fire? Who?* The fire Captain did not share any details or theories as to the fire's origin.

As I listen to the news report, my chest starts to tighten. I think about holding a meeting of the board members. *That's exactly what they're counting on.* I know that if I react (to what they only see as a competitor getting ushered out of the way), then they would surely have even less respect for me. Sooner or later, they would figure out a way to take me out of the CEO seat.

My hands are tied.

My desk phone rings, and I rush to it, partly hoping that it is going to be Alexandra. But I know that is highly unlikely.

She's going to think I did this, I think to myself as I reach for the phone. She's going to resent me even more.

"Hello." I say, trying not to sound too enthusiastic.

"Sir, Megan Frost from The Daily Journal on line two for you," my secretary tells me.

Deflated, I respond, "Tell her I have no comment. I'll be taking no interviews for now." I slam the phone back into its berth, angry that it wasn't Alexandra's voice on the other end.

Reporters are likely already circling, looking for a story. I know this is all part of their big plan in search of their big scoop. I don't doubt that I'll have to talk to them at some point.

It wouldn't surprise me if some lofty reporter will force some connection between Alexandra and I dating, and the fire. Some analysts could hint there would be losses incurred at Seth BioTech. They could point to the pictures of Alexandra and I together. Assumptions would be made that because of our relationship, Brent-Sigma could swoop in and save the day, with the price of Seth BioTech shares, of course.

Richard and his crew had this planned from the start, I am starting to believe. And I handed them the extra detail that they needed on a silver platter. I can't openly go against them now. They don't deserve the satisfaction. Or the power.

But, I can talk with Alexandra.

Without further thought (and so that I won't change my mind), I grab my jacket and head straight for the parking lot, then head for Seth BioTech.

Driving over to the fire, I wonder about what I am going to say to her that will make any sense. *I wouldn't even believe me,* I think to myself. I know convincing her that I had nothing to do with the fire is a far stretch, but I still have to try to talk with her.

I also know I am taking a big risk going to Seth BioTech in the first place. It is both going against Richard's plans and playing into them. If he finds out later that I went to the fire to see Alexandra, he would definitely try to spin the story in favor of booting me out of the CEO's chair.

Nonetheless, when I arrive, the fire trucks and other first responder vehicles are in the process of leaving. I bring my car to a halt three buildings away. I don't want the Press to see me there.

I take off my jacket, roll up my sleeves and put on a baseball cap before I get out of the car. Sneaking past the lights, the cameras, and the bustle of everything, I manage to find my way to a security guard who is standing, looking up at the building.

"Excuse me, sir." I ask him. He looks up at me, with a faint spark of recognition. "Can you please bring me to Alexandra Seth?"

"I don't know what to tell you, man. You came at a really bad time." *Captain Obvious*. But, something about him tells me he is a nice guy who just wants to do the right thing.

"Hey look. I promise I'm not a reporter, I'm her friend. Just here to see if she's alright and offer her my support. If you bring me to her, you'll see that she knows me. I want to help her tonight if she needs my help." I flash him a look to say I am sincere. But it also maybe says that I'm not going anywhere until I get what I want.

"Follow me, sir." Thankfully, he doesn't take too much time to ponder a decision. He turns around and leads me to her.

When I see the hatred on Alexandra's face, the tightening in my chest gets stronger, as if completely blocking out my airway. She lunges to punch at me, but her coworker stops her. I try to get out the words that I had nothing to do with the fire, but there is too much commotion between us and her coworker tries to calm her down. Anyway, I wouldn't believe me if I were her.

What I could tell her sounds absurd to me. I had nothing to do with the sabotage, but somehow I also knew everything about it. After all, I have an idea that some at Brent-Sigma are tied to the fire. I can look back at conversations and occurrences these past two days and believe that I know who played a part. But as much as it pains me, I can't tell her mere theories until I have proof. I need to handle it quietly, before they cross another line.

When I walk away from Alexandra, it is because it's what she says she wants. But, I immediately start to think about how I am going to get the proof she needs and that I didn't know anything about the fire. I also realize that it is more important, however, to figure out who started the fire. I know it has to be someone inside Seth BioTech.

So, when I am out of sight of Alexandra and her two co-workers, I step behind a parked vehicle and keep watch until her coworkers leave, and she remains standing alone. Looking at the burnt building.

I move up beside Alexandra, facing the building. "I'm not done yet."

"You lied to me," she slips the words through her gritting teeth. "You had every chance to tell me the truth about who you were, but you didn't. You took me to bed while you were trying to sabotage my research. Ha! I fell for it, hook, line, and sinker. What a stupid, desperate fool I am. I expect as much from Brent-Sigma."

Let her speak. Let her say all she wants to say. The only way I might possibly be able to get through to her is if I listen to her first.

"I never lied to you," I let out, meekly. While that was logically true, I did lie to her. By using my omission of the whole truth as some excuse for why I did what I did, I was selling her short. "No, I'm sorry. Of course… What I mean…"

"Right," she interrupts, already having comprehended the situation. "You just left out the most important part about yourself; being the CEO of the company that is trying to buy out mine. Big, powerful, all-important Ellis Brent. Mister bigshot extraordinaire. The family business, my fucking ass. You left out 'The family Empire'. That would have been the truth. The fucking global pharmaceutical company that wants to…" She trails off, swallowing the rest of her thoughts.

Fumes of frustration and gloom seem to replace the words that are left unsaid. Her look of helpless disappointment sear into my brain.

She can't say it, but I know what she is thinking. Those words. The thought racing through her mind. The whole reason why I couldn't tell her who I am. *It is my company that has designs on hers. To swallow Seth BioTech bite by bite, then chew it up into unrecognizable pieces.*

The way she is talking and the look on her face. She is disgusted just looking at me.

She runs her hands over her hair, to the ponytail holder tying her hair in back. Then she bends over and picks up pieces of charred petri dishes that had melted into one another. I am holding on to hope that she is stuck between believing me and thinking I am to blame. That way, at least there's a chance.

Finally, she speaks. "Do you see these?" She raises the charred petri dishes high between us so that I can see the melted plastic mixed with black soot.

"Tracey had these in her hands when I found her tonight. She was in shock and had this look of despair on her face. I know exactly what she was feeling. Shock. Because she made it out alive. And, by the way, she had the wherewithal to pull the fire alarm so that others could get out of the building safely as well. But, mostly. Despair. We are feeling Despair." I am floored with feelings of sadness and helplessness when I see the corners of her mouth turn unnaturally downward and tears pooling in her eyes.

"Let me ask you something, Ellis." She brings the charred remains down and then continues. "Did you for once think about how many more people could be saved if you had only just let this go? These petri dishes represent the absolute, crushing Despair that I feel knowing that all the work I've been doing for the better half of this year, and for my whole life, was destroyed. Burned to a melted, wasted crisp in a matter of minutes."

Alexandra takes a step away from me. "I could probably have forgiven you for lying to me about who you are. But to be so thoughtless and have no care for all these people's lives." Alexandra waves the plastic, dark, lumpy mess up towards me.

She looks at me with cheerless and miserable eyes that I will never forget, and says, "This, I will never forgive you for."

**

Those words. They are thousands of splinters pushing deep into my heart. Her anger. Her disappointment in the person she thinks I am. She has every right to question me. To question my intentions.

She stands for a while, staring towards her damaged office building. Finally, she speaks weakly. "You aren't from Brent-Sigma, you are Brent-Sigma."

It occurs to me that this could be my opportunity to help her understand why I couldn't tell her my identity right away. "Yes. You're right. But, I hope that all of this shows why I couldn't figure out the best way to tell you who___"

"Why are you even here, Ellis?" She turns to me, interrupting my explanation. "To gloat? To take one last glance at what you accomplished?" She turns her hand, palm up, and waves it toward the smoking building. "Well, there you go. Everything you've wanted, wrapped up in a smoldering, fucking bow!"

"That's not … it wasn't … how can you even think that?" I ask, even though she has every reason to think that. "Look, I mean I do know you have good reasons. But, I couldn't figure out how to tell you that I'm Ellis Brent." I try to grab her hands in mine, but she pulls them quickly away and crosses her arms in front.

I try to continue. "Look, if I had told you my name at the coffee shop, you would have asked me if I was connected to Brent-Sigma. When I told you, don't you agree that you would have had nothing to do with me? You wouldn't have given me a chance."

121

Instead of an answer, she stands silently. Face straight, with no reaction.

I can understand why she might feel as if I don't deserve an answer. However, she is letting me talk. So, I continue.

"That day, I knew exactly who you were, right when I walked into the coffee shop. I could only see the side of your face when you were in line, but we were talking about Seth BioTech at my office, and I was researching you right before we met." Finally, I'm telling the truth. Although now that I am telling it, she has every reason to be even angrier with me.

"So, I did recognize you." I am hoping that my words are matched with the sincere look that I am attempting to portray. "I was immediately struck. Mesmerized. In my head, I was thinking, 'Turn around Ellis. Don't do it. Walk away. What the hell are you thinking?' But, I just wanted to talk to you."

"There were moments at the coffee shop when I thought that you must have known who I was. Like when you made that joke about me meeting women at the coffee shop. I thought you might have known about my playboy reputation." Ugh, I'm all over the place. I want to be able to tell her everything so that she can see I'm trying to be open. But I also don't want to make more of a mess of things by adding negative ideas about me in her mind.

"And I admit. At first, I did have thoughts run through my mind that I could gather company intel if I talked to you. That maybe you'd end up being a sour bitch and we'd have good reason to buy into your company." I see hints of anger rise on her face, so I rush to make my point before she can speak out. "But you are who you are, and you're not a sour bitch. You don't deserve what my company wanted to do to yours. And you don't deserve this." I point towards the burnt building.

"Alexandra, I fell for you the moment I met you. And I just wanted to keep learning more. Getting to know you." I am hoping that my words are making some small dent in her being able to believe me. "All the time we spent together; it was real for me. But, I couldn't figure out a way to tell you who I was without you wanting to have nothing to do with me. And, I was selfish. Because all I wanted was more time."

"Please believe me when I say that I had nothing to do with the fire. I didn't know about it, nor did I have an idea that anyone had plans to do something like this. Please tell me you don't think I did this." I plead with her, hoping she has heard what I'm saying and that she believes me.

She looks up at me. Those grey eyes, catching the light from the moon, possibly revealing her search for truth or sincerity anywhere within my eyes. I am hoping what I see is that she believes me. But, it is probably just hope.

"I don't know what to think," she finally replies, as she tosses the charred petri dishes in her hand to the ground. As if to show me, or remind me, that they now mean nothing. "If you care for me the way you say, then hear this." She pauses briefly to emphasize the next dagger to my heart.

"Leave."

Chapter Eight

Alexandra

Wednesday

There is nothing else I can do at this moment. On this night. Nothing that staring at the charred exterior of Seth BioTech can accomplish. Knowing that it is not just charred, but the lab and all the work done inside are destroyed.

Ellis Brent. My instinct tells me I need to figure out how to prove he had something to do with the fire. It has to be him. But the more I replay our conversations and the Ellis that I got to know, the more I can convince myself that he is not the enemy.

I also want to believe it wasn't him. *Of course you want to believe he had nothing to do with the fire. You weak, fucking sap.* I am being tough on myself. But I deserve it. I let this man into my heart. Into my fucking house. My bed. Thoughts of being tangled with him. The sound of my name on his lips. "Alexandra."

Snap out of it, princess. I have to tell myself. Angry, because just the thought of Ellis breathing my name is sending shocks through my body.

OK, what do I need to do to switch into thinking mode and figure out what to do next? I am trying to process this overload of emotions, thoughts, ideas, and the knowledge that decisions and choices need to be made about Seth BioTech.

Starting over begins tomorrow. For both me and my company.

When I get into my car, I feel the urge to slam the door closed, but I put my rage in check and close it slowly instead. It feels like everything in me is hanging on by a thin thread.

I grip the steering wheel, tightening, until my hands start to hurt. That thin thread I thought was there has already ripped, and I don't know what I'm hanging onto. My eyes are filled, my face wet with tears.

Heaviness. My bones weigh me down into the seat of my car. Then, a realization.

In this moment, it doesn't matter to me whether I believe him. I want to see him. To sit and talk with him. Maybe I'll be able to tell if he is lying or telling the truth.

If it's true that he's fallen for me. I could use that to my advantage.

I am just wasting time thinking about whether to contact him. If I spend too much time thinking, I am pretty sure I'll eventually convince myself against it. So, I pick up my cell phone and just call him.

Ellis picks up my call before I hear the second ring. The second I hear his voice, I know that I want to believe that he had no part in sabotaging my lab. As we talk, I start to realize that hearing him over the phone isn't going to be enough. Even just hearing his apologies, I can feel myself thinking that he is telling the truth.

I can't just easily fall for his lies again.

I think that I need to see him. Face-to-face. That way I will be able to look him in his eyes and read his body language. That will tell me more than the flowery, apologetic, sad-sounding words I am listening to come through the cell phone.

Plus, even if he wasn't the one behind the fire, it still doesn't mean he didn't know about plans to destroy my lab, I remind myself.

"I need to see you. Let's talk this out face-to-face so that you can explain everything to me." I do hope that I sound generous in my allowing him to see me, but also firm and guarded.

His voice, though, sounds relieved and grateful. As if he sees this as an opportunity to convince me of his lies and instantly forgive him. "Thank you, Alexandra. Yes. I want to see you too. Please let me explain and tell you everything I can. I'm so sorry for lying to you and I want to make this up to you. I *hope* I can make this up to you."

Actually, no. That's not what I want. I don't want to hear his excuses and what I'll just hear as being made-up explanations. I'm not meeting up with him so that he can attempt to pry his way into my heart.

"Let's be clear, Ellis, this is not the first stop on your apology tour." I need to set expectations right away so that there is no confusion about why I am agreeing to meet him. "I'm only giving you the chance to explain what you feel you need to. That's all. Nothing more."

We agree to meet at a quiet dive bar that he knows of in a sleepy town, on the backroads, southeast of Sacramento. It is out of the way for me, but it is definitely the kind of place where no one would recognize us.

The entire drive to the bar, I am going over questions in my mind for what I feel I need to know from him. There are too many questions, though, where I am starting to feel my emotions heighten.

Like, 'If you knew that you wanted to stop your company from buying into mine, why didn't you just ghost me after the coffee shop?'

Instead of setting up our date at Notre Terre, he could have just allowed me to leave the coffee shop and let me go on with my day. After stopping his company's interest in mine, he could have reached out later and found me again if he was still interested.

Or, 'Even if he did intend to stop the buyout, why wasn't one of his options to let me know when we were at the diner?' I know he would have had to tell me everything, but if he really cared about me then letting me in on his plans could have been an option. I think about this some more.

What *would* have been my reaction to him telling me his real name? That he is *the* Ellis Brent, CEO at Brent-Sigma. I admit to myself that if he'd told me anytime during the first day that we met, I would have signed him off. That would have been the last time I would have spent time alone with him again. *At least until the threat from Brent-Sigma was gone.*

I already understood why he didn't tell me the truth on that first day. And the more I thought about it, I could see why he wouldn't have offered the truth since it meant I'd walk away. Especially if I didn't know who he was and if he really was interested in me right away (the way he said he was).

The thought that this proved he really fell for me the first moment he met me releases butterflies in my gut. *Wow Alexandra. And if you really think that, then you are pathetic. He lied to me because he liked me so much.* Not a top character quality I usually look for in a partner.

OK, what if he would have told me the truth the next day, what would my reaction have been? While I do know that my initial reaction would have been to freak and lash out, I wonder if I would have calmed down, eventually. *He should have come clean when we were at the diner.*

I am still driving to meet Ellis and I continue to process the questions I have for him. I'm taking mental notes, putting into two columns those questions that are just for informational purposes and those that make me feel extra emotions. When I drive up to the dive bar, I waste no time and walk right in.

Whoever designed the interior of the bar really liked wood. Oak, to be exact. Wood floors, wood paneling on the walls, wood doors and window frames, and a long wood bar that spans the entire length of one side of the room. Four sets of tables and chairs, all wood, sit opposite the bar. Just a jukebox with a frame of neon lighting is set apart from everything else at the far end of the bar. The smell of wood, alcohol, and mop water permeates the single room.

I drop off my sweatshirt at a table with three chairs at the end of the room, closest to the jukebox. There really isn't a better choice. All the windows are by the bar entrance, and from the jukebox area I can see anyone who comes in through the door. People can pass by this table when they want to use the restroom or choose songs on the jukebox. But seeing as there are only three other people in the bar, I don't worry much about feeling crowded.

I walk up to the bar and the bartender comes over, asking, "What can I get ya?"

Just a handful of options on the shelves behind the bartender makes my choice easy. "Rye. Neat. With a glass of ice."

"Whoa, nice." Ellis remarks as he walks up to stand next to me at the bar. "One hell of a night, huh?"

"Exactly," I reply, staring straight ahead. "My night has been hell," I say icily. I don't want to give him the satisfaction of knowing his presence is having an effect on me. His enticing trademark of musk and sandalwood announces his entrance, even before I answer his question. If I turn my head to look into his eyes, I know my face will betray me.

"Showing up at my company like that...your board members must have been really annoyed." I leave my card with the bartender when he brings my drink and take my glass of whiskey and glass of ice to the table.

"Trailhead draft please." He tells the bartender when asked for his order.

Ellis turns around to address me at the table, "Yes, well, they're not going to find out because I was never there."

As he finishes his transaction with the bartender, I process his meaning. I wonder if there is anything he can tell me that won't garner doubt and suspicion in anything he says to me.

When he sits down at the table, in the chair across from me, I hold his gaze for a while. Gauging how I might interpret his demeanor.

I take in the sight of him. He is dressed in khaki pants and a baby blue polo shirt. His eyes still look the same as they did before, except their emerald pools seem darkened. They stare back at me with concern, sincerity, care, and hope.

Pathetic, I think about myself as I feel a softening towards him. He's all wrapped up in a handsome package that I have to fight myself to not be lured into bed with.

Finally, I let out, "Was any of it real?" As soon as I ask this question, I want to kick myself. I know it isn't what I had wanted to start with. The whole drive over, I was creating a mental list of questions that I had broken into two lists: those based on emotion (that I was convinced would be a waste of time) and those that were going straight for the facts.

Instead, the question at the top of that Emotional list, was the one that came flying out of my mouth. Without reason or control.

"All of it was real," he responds immediately. "I swear to you Alexandra when I confess that I fell for you the moment I saw you, it is 100% the truth. The reason why I couldn't tell you who I was, was because I knew you wouldn't have given me a chance if you knew the truth right away."

I lift my hand to stop him. "That's not the question I wanted to ask." I insist. "I don't even know you. So whatever answer you give, I won't believe you." I feel a wave of accomplishment seeing a pained look flash across his face and observing that it looks like I hurt him.

He adjusts the apologetic tone from his voice and says, "I understand where you're coming from. I want to help you with anything you need to know to help us get past …" I can tell that he is going to say 'this', but he stops himself. It looks like he remembers that the purpose of his meeting with me isn't so he can apologize and I can forgive him. It is only for me to get to the truth.

"What do you want to know?" he asks instead.

I am watching his gestures, his eyes, and facial expressions so that I can gather the whole picture of what is behind the words he's telling me. He is offering me access to his life on a platter. *How are you so sure he's not just going to lie again?* I can't be sure, but I owe it to myself to see what I can find out.

"You already told me on our first date about growing up in El Dorado Hills and you went to college in Santa Clara. Were you in the military?" I ask.

"After I got my degree I went through the Marine's Officers program. My current rank is Captain, 1st Marine Division." He replies, without flinching. His eyes hold fast on mine.

"So you have killed people?" Impressed with myself that I am maintaining a cool and steady composure, I then notice a look on his face that tells me I have struck a nerve with that question. He looks over at me and it seems like he is starting to erect walls around that topic. He parts his lips to speak but lets out just a breath before closing his mouth.

So he has a hard time talking about the Marines. Does it really matter to my situation at hand? I decide that the answer doesn't concern me at this time, and I am all right with moving on.

"Never mind. When did you get back?" My next question causes a look of relief to wash over him. He is happy to change the subject.

"Just over a month ago. You may have heard about the car crash that killed both my parents in June?" This memory should still reside close to his heart since it happened just 4 months ago. If he can share this difficult information, I might be able to reach those vulnerable pieces within him.

"I did," I let him know softly. "I'm sorry. Although different circumstances, I also know the heartbreak of losing a parent."

"It's all right, thank you." He answers back. "I'm an only child."

We both take sips from our drinks. I watch as sadness creeps over his face. The fact that I am also an only child pops into my mind, but I snap an imaginary clip over my lips. This talk isn't about me or helping him to feel better.

When it feels like an appropriate amount of time to let him process his last statement, I continue with my questioning.

"So, you just took over the running of your family company about a month ago. Right?" He nods his head in confirmation. *This is why I didn't know you. I've been so entrenched in research and development for the last five months.*

"I must seem like an idiot to you, not knowing who you were. After all, I'm the CTO and Founder of my company. I should know the big news surrounding all our competitors. At least know about the people running those companies. Especially the company threatening to buy us out."

He interrupts me. "No Alexandra. I could never think you're an idiot. Look, at the coffee shop when I asked you what you did, you didn't say your actual title. You told me that you were a scientist. I saw the look of satisfaction, no, pride on your face when you owned that part of you. It was obvious that the science is where your heart and your focus is. I thought that might have something to do with why you didn't recognize me. But I could only let myself feel excited that I had a chance to get to know you."

He looks up and sees that I am shutting down again. I am not there to hear about how he has feelings for me.

I don't doubt that a look of dissatisfaction crosses over my face because he stops talking. I stand up and wave at the bartender. "Same, please," I tell him. He pours me a new drink and he brings two glasses back to the table, taking my empty ones.

Ellis continues, seeming to be catching on to the purpose of this meeting. "So, it was almost time for me to re-enlist in the Marines when my parents died. I was all set to continue my military service because I had found another family. I finally had brothers and sisters. We were bonded in life. And death." He stares into blank space for a while before he continues speaking to me.

"That must have been hard; leaving like that. How do you feel about being CEO?" I ask.

"I enjoy both worlds," he responds. Then he smiles again, the bright emerald in his green eyes returning, focusing on me. "There was a time when I wanted to run my family's company more than anything. I observed and studied to become the best of the best. I wanted to learn every area that was concerned with the smooth running of the company—I'm talking the bringing together of compounds to make a drug, the packaging of that drug, the distribution, the legal, the marketing…"

I smile as he speaks because I understand what he means in the way of being passionate about what you're doing and how that can bring you joy. Although he doesn't deserve to know, I can't help but to enjoy this side of him.

"And now?" I inquire. "Do you still enjoy your job at Brent-Sigma?"

He doesn't answer this question and instead raises his beer to his lips. Thinking. Then his eyes meet mine. "It really hurt me when you thought I sabotaged your lab. You know how much I respect your work."

"I believed it at the coffee shop when you said you did. Now I have no reason to believe anything you say." This is an obvious statement, spoken out loud more so to remind myself and any part of me that is softening to him.

"Why were you trying to buy my company out then?" I ask.

"That morning before the coffee shop, we had a meeting about buying shares of Seth BioTech. And what we planned to do after that purchase. I think I told you earlier that I was researching you as well. I was all in for the plan." *Finally*, he's telling me the truth.

"Then I met you and suddenly I questioned the purchase." He has learned during our time here at the bar that I'm not looking for validation. So he changes course. "And look, I know you don't want to hear that I fell for you and changed my mind. So I'll spare you that detail."

"I'll just say that I changed my mind." He continues. "After the coffee shop, I went back to the office and one of the lead board members came in to talk to me. He was there to make sure that I was 100% in on buying shares of your company." I feel myself flinch and hope he didn't see it.

"I suggested to him that we could maybe look somewhere other than Seth BioTech. He just laughed at me." Searching his eyes and looking for signs of deception, I am shocked when I hear his words and don't see those signs.

"When I left your house the next morning before the sun came up, it wasn't because I wanted to leave. I needed to get back to Brent-Sigma and redirect our mission." He has a newfound determination that locks into his eyes. I sense he thinks he is getting somewhere with me.

"I already had the generalized plan for our new direction in mind. So, the first thing I did was to call a board meeting. I told everyone that the Seth BioTech deal was dead in the water. We were not going to pursue your company. Ever. They didn't like to hear that, but I told them that we needed to keep up with the times and come up with new innovations of our own. We were no longer creating new medicines. So for our own strength and longevity, I suggested that we go back to what made us big in the first place. New drugs and advancements in medicine."

While Ellis is speaking, the bartender walks up and makes a sign towards his watch-less wrist that it's closing time. He sets down the bill and has Ellis sign for the tab. The bartender places my card on the table, without a bill, and pushes my card toward me. Apparently, Ellis is covering both of our drinks and I don't care. After the bartender walks away, Ellis and I do not speak.

I am processing everything I have just heard. A tear that had welled up in my eye skips down my cheek and I shake it off, wiping my hand across attempting to disguise its appearance. I didn't realize that I was feeling upset or even angry – and that makes me a bit upset and angry at myself.

Ellis places his hand on mine. It is warm and coarse. Strong, yet light. I inadvertently catch another whiff of his musk after taking in a much-needed breath. A familiar wave of ecstasy sweeps up my spine.

Don't do it, Alexandra. My brain is telling me to keep my senses. But, my body wants to be with him. I want to feel light again.

Do I really need to have all the answers tonight? As I sit there, looking into his eyes, my mind and body forge an inner battle. Fighting to gain control. My mind; fighting for my sanity, self-respect, ideals, and reason. My body; countering with the argument that I could use this moment to take control of what I want and how I want it – keeping my sanity, self-respect, ideals, and reason intact.

"Are you alright?" he asks, looking into my eyes. He must have noticed me looking at him funny. "You've had a lot to drink. I'm going to drive you home."

Neither disagreeing with nor fighting his decision, I simply reply, "Ellis. You can drive my car and bring me home. And then you can get yours in the morning." I follow him outside, arms crossed in front of me.

Chapter Nine

Ellis

Wednesday

A lexandra falls asleep in the passenger seat as soon as I start driving to her house.

I look over at her beautiful sleeping face and wonder if I had made any leeway in getting through to her. It had been my hope that if I just answered all her questions, then she'd see in my eyes that I do want to tell her the truth from now on. I want her to know she can trust me.

Thoughts swim through my mind, wondering what she wants me to do when I bring her to her house. *Would she want me to go inside with her? Would I be disrespecting her if I did, knowing how vulnerable she could be tonight?* Of course, I want to stay with her. I know that if I get the chance to stay, I will not want to leave again.

When I drive up to Alexandra's house, I park her car in the driveway, turn off the engine, and gently whisper, "Hey, we're here. You're home, Alexandra."

Her eyes flutter open, staring at me for a moment before she turns and opens her car door.

I step out of the car, hand her the keys, and walk her up to the front door.

"Thank you for meeting up with me tonight and giving me a chance to talk with you. I hope you'll call me if there's anything else you want to know from me. I'm here for you." I say, trying not to sound like I am pleading or expecting too much from her.

She looks at me but doesn't say anything. Her look makes me think, *I don't deserve her forgiveness*. I know that much.

Then she turns around to open her front door, walks inside, and closes the door behind her. A second later, I hear the bolt latch and the porch light turns off.

Having the door closed on me and standing in the dark feels harsh. I look all around and notice there are no streetlamps in this neighborhood. *I deserved that,* I think to myself. I reach into my pocket, pull out my cell phone, and open my rideshare app.

While I schedule a ride back to my car at the dive bar, I wonder what else I can do to make inroads with Alexandra. What more does she want from me? I'm ready to answer all her questions. But I can't do anything if she won't talk to me.

My phone buzzes and I see that my ride is scheduled. *"Peter" is coming in 25 minutes.*

I step down from Alexandra's porch and take a seat on the second step.

The only thing I can do from here is fix things on my end and secure the safety of Alexandra's company from mine. So, first thing in the morning I'll check in to see whether the board made any movement towards creating a new plan for Brent-Sigma's company direction. I know that I actively need to be elbows deep into crafting our strategy and goals for how to move Brent-Sigma into the 21st century and rebuild it into the innovator that it once was. Thinking about the possibilities, I feel a new sense of inspiration and determination.

I look down at my phone. According to the app, Peter, my rideshare is 2 minutes away. I stand up, brush off my pants, and start walking to the curb.

When I get to about a few yards from the street, I hear the bolt from Alexandra's front door slide open and I stop to turn around to see Alexandra standing in her doorway.

"Is everything all right?" I call back to her.

The lights in her home form an aura around her body as they light up from behind her. The darkness of everything outside her home keeps her face in shadows. I can't decide whether I should stay put or walk back towards her.

After a couple of seconds, and not receiving an answer from her, I start to walk back towards her house. Immediately she holds up her hand and says, "Stop, Ellis." I halt in my tracks, waiting for her to speak again.

She doesn't say anything, and I turn my head when I see a flash of headlights turn the corner onto her street.

"If there's anything you need, let me know. I don't expect anything, but if you want to talk some more, I will stay or... I don't know. It's your call. Just let me know what you want from me Alexandra and I'll do it."

The dark sedan with a rideshare light on the dashboard stops on the street in front of Alexandra's house.

"Just let me know what you need." I point back to the car to show that I am taking the ride. "I have to go. Goodbye."

I head towards my rideshare and greet the driver through the open window of the front passenger door.

What am I doing? If I get into the car now and drive away, I would officially be the world's biggest idiot. "Peter, I'll pay and give you a great tip. But, I won't need a ride right now." He looks around me towards the house, seeming to understand my meaning, nods, and thanks me, then closes his window and drives away.

I turn around to see that Alexandra is still standing in her doorway. I walk towards her and stand in front of her on the front porch. This time she doesn't stop me.

"I don't need you." Her first words spoken to me since opening her door and watching me send my rideshare away. "You being in my life, doesn't change who I am."

"No, of course not. You…"

"I'm not finished." She cuts me short. Still not moving from her position in the frame of her door.

"You have really hurt me. I don't see us the same way now, in the hopeful way I saw us when we were on our movie date." Since I am standing just a couple of feet from her, I can see her face. Her expression tells me she is thinking about her words

147

and calculating the best way to communicate them. I wait in silence for her direction.

"I don't need you. But---," she pauses a moment, breathes in and exhales then steps down to me from her doorway. "In this moment, I want you. I want you to come with me inside and let me have you. With no expectations, no promises. No talk about what we will do next. Just …" She heaves in another deep breath in, then out. "The only choice I give you in this moment is, you can call another rideshare and leave, or you can stay but you will leave before morning."

I step forward to move into her space and say, "I will stay now. I want to stay. And will leave when you tell me." I offer my mouth to her, and she accepts by parting her lips and allowing me to press in for a deep, hungry kiss. My left hand moves to the small of her back, bringing her body in, next to mine. My other hand grabs her by the hair next to the nape of her neck, pulling her mouth closer to mine. Letting me kiss her hard and with purpose.

I try to be both gentle and forceful. Lifting her up from the ground and walking us forward into her home. Our lips remain locked as if we both are being carried by their connection. It feels like nothing can fit between us. I am the one physically moving her body with mine into the house, but it is as if it were her lips carrying me, holding me to her.

A question crosses my mind and I pull away from her. My lips feel the ache to keep kissing hers and the longing in my body feels like a tidal wave, ready to crash onto the shore. I have tasted her, and I want it all. Before we go further, I must look into her eyes and find out, "Are you sure?" I ask.

She looks at me, lips red from the pressure against mine. Her eyes glaring, suggesting that stopping wasn't easy for her either. I hope that it was difficult. I like thinking that she can't wait to be with me again, to breathe me in. Because I feel the same exact way.

"Shut up Ellis and bring me to bed."

Chapter Ten

Alexandra

Wednesday/Thursday, Middle of the Night

I am hungry for him. It is not just an ache that I feel. Wanting him. Desiring him. These are wanton feelings that I need fulfilled. These are pains from starvation. Of not allowing myself the one thing that will curb my appetite. Him.

When I turn the lock of my deadbolt and turn off the porchlight, I remain standing. Facing my front door. My feet planted in place, rooted to the floor. Slowly, I bend my neck to release my head forward. When my forehead reaches the wood of the door, I feel my body relax and give in to the anchor that my skin to the wood provides.

Deep breath in. Release.

He is right on the other side of this door. Even though I'm not looking through my peephole and don't actually know whether he is still there, I sense that I can feel his energy through the wood that separates us. I want him.

My heart is fractured because of him. A thousand fault lines mar my heavily guarded heart. Yet, I also give myself credit to know that I'm strong enough to get through any broken heart. I've been through pain, heartbreak, and extreme sorrow. I know what it means to lose someone who means the most. Someone who was the most...

This hurts like hell. I think to myself, doing a body scan to assess where it is that I am hurting. And while I wouldn't be surprised if all the bones in my body were broken, I recognize from the phantom ache in my chest and the annoying lump in my throat, that I am just fine. *It only sucks. That's it. It just plain sucks.*

I can get what I need right now, and it doesn't mean I'm weak. There would be nothing wrong with just having sex tonight. But what if he expects more? What if it confuses me? What if it confuses him? It should be easy enough to just have sex. My mind is racing in circles, rapid-firing arguments for and against opening the door to Ellis and offering meaningless sex.

With each passing second, I have still not found a conclusion or decision. If anything, I find that the longer I stand there in thought, the emptier my mind feels. *I either need to open this door or walk upstairs.* Having only two options, I think, will make it easier for my body to move from my current state. And in this moment of indecision, a decision made is a good decision.

My mindless fingers unlock the deadbolt and open the door.

***

Sex. Is. Fucking. Glorious.

It is somewhat different this time. Still intense. All-consuming. Everywhere he touches, my mind and body feel. I am a collection of shudders and waves. Sounds, and breaths held in.

This time, in addition to exchanging kisses and movements that are ravenous and greedy, I also feel a tenderness that I had not felt our first time together. It is as if Ellis wants to make sure that I am feeling pleasure. As if he is going to stay until I am not holding anything back.

I test this theory. Grabbing and stroking him in ways I know would make most men finish quickly. Before Ellis gets too far, he grabs me and changes positions so that he can return the favor. Licking my neck, trailing his tongue south, between my breasts and down to my navel. I moan with pleasure, knowing that the sound of my gratification will increase his.

Trying again, I pull him up so that we can kiss. Tongues battling for dominance, or submission. As we kiss, I sway my hips underneath him, feeling him hard with anticipation. He presses pause on my play by putting his hand under my right knee, and pulling it up, opening my legs so that he can move down and start fresh kisses beginning at my knee and moving in between my legs.

Let him, I say to myself. *This is why I wanted him to stay.* Instead of thinking I have the power only if I can control his pleasure, I decide that I have the most power when I give in to my own.

I grab a tuft of hair on the top of his head and pull his head down between my legs, letting him indulge my every whim. And when I know I am nearing my edge of no going back, I pull him back up to me. "I want you now." I moan.

He moves up to kiss me, his mouth and tongue doused in my womanhood. Sharing his discovery with me. Letting me taste myself.

I can't wait, I think, so I slide my hand down to grab his throbbing manhood and guide him into me. "Ohhhhh," escapes from my lips as he enters me and starts to move in and out, one hand supporting my head on the pillow, the other holding my leg.

We are still kissing so when we moan we can feel our voices travel through our bodies, paving a fiery path. I take my hand and pull his head away with a tuft of hair. "Harder," I beg.

Ellis provides one compliant thrust, then slides off to my right. His mouth still demanding possession over mine. With his hands on my hips, he moves me to face away from him, then uses one hand to part my legs and insert his hardness into me from behind.

"Holy, fuck, yes!" These words that escape my lips mean exactly what I am experiencing.

He wraps my hair at the nape of my neck around his bottom hand and yanks slightly, pulling my head back to him, giving him control and access for his mouth to have its will over my neck and my ear. Sucking and kissing, licking and biting.

My request is then satisfied as he holds my hair and leg and drives into me with the energetic and potent thrusts that I had asked for.

After a while he slows down, it crosses my mind that if he continues then he'll finish before me. So, I adjust my hips to allow myself to better position my hand between my legs while he continues to move behind me.

He immediately takes my hand and moves it up to his mouth. Tasting my fingers. Still sucking my finger in his mouth, his hand then moves to replace mine between my legs.

All my untamed sensations are firing and emitting from every inch of me. Feeling his body respond, communicating to me that his pleasure mirrors mine. Hearing the confirmation that that is true in the sounds that escape his lips.

I climb and ascend. Closer and closer. Then. As his touch and our movements send me over the edge and towards its anticipated purpose, I scream, "Ellis!" And my body seizes in pleasure-laden waves while I feel his body follow with its own climax and release. The crests and troughs of my orgasm rewarding him, still inside me. Pulling out anything remaining from his own blissful conclusion.

A few minutes later, I move from underneath him and get up to use the bathroom. After cleaning up, I look in the mirror while washing my hands.

The woman staring back at me is fulfilled and in control of all her faculties. *I am still Alexandra Seth. I am still my kick-ass self.* And whether these feelings of strength and empowerment are because of some post-sex euphoria, doesn't matter to me. I know my worth and can still be proud of myself and everything that is important to me.

I step back into my room and find Ellis lying on his back on my bed. Sleeping.

I leave him alone and walk quietly down the stairwell to the kitchen.

On the counter is the glass of Petite Sirah that I had poured just hours before when I received Tracey's call about the fire. I grab the stem, remove the plastic wrap, and sniff. I savor the smell of fat, red wine.

I take a sip and walk over to my living room and sit in an armchair looking out a window to my backyard.

This is a good time to sit and just think. When the outside world is quiet and not demanding anything from you in return.

When was the last time I felt like this? I think about this question but cannot come up with the answer.

While various thoughts about Ellis cross my mind, I try to redirect them to just thoughts about myself. Feeling content and not burdened with anything going on outside my house.

I hear Ellis's footsteps near as he comes down the stairs and into my view, wearing only boxer briefs. Our eyes meet and he smiles. I smile back, but with returned composure.

There is tension in the room—the tension between us—it is still present. There is a finality that looms over us, like we know what is going to happen so there is no need to rush into conversation. But the strange thing is, I have no idea what is going to happen. The hairs on my body stand at attention when he walks into the living room.

"Do you want to be alone, or do you want company?" He asks. His eyes are on me as I lift my empty wine glass and point to the bottle of wine on the counter. He takes my glass from me and walks over to refill it with wine.

He flashes me a grin on his way back to me, also carrying with him the bottle of wine. He takes a sip from my glass, before handing it back to me. Kneeling on one knee beside my seat.

"I believe you." I start to say. Feeling like this moment, in the middle of the night, without the weight of the world on my shoulders, is the best time for this talk. "I believe your feelings for me, your reasons for not telling me the truth, that you were trying to stop the buyout, and that you didn't know about the fire."

Even though Ellis's eyes gleam with the acknowledgment that I believe him, I can also see from his look that he is reading my expression and he understands what I have not yet said.

I take a sip of wine and then offer Ellis my glass. He drinks in a long gulp and then pours more wine into the glass before handing it back to me.

"Is it time for me to leave?" He asks while he lifts his hand to stroke my knee. His face is mere inches from mine.

I move my head to his, my nose brushing his cheek. With my eyes closed, I breathe in a long slow breath, taking in the scent of sandalwood and sex. I open my mouth to gently taste his face, lost in wonder as to whether I might taste the carnal scent. When he moves barely a millimeter, I stop him. Whispering with my eyes still shut, "Yes. It's time for you to go."

Chapter Eleven

Ellis

Thursday

After the night Alexandra and I spent together, I hated that I had to go home to my own bed. I especially hated the feeling of waking up without her next to me. I'm up before the sun has reared its head out of the clouds and I feel like my bed is as uninviting as a nest of thorns.

The smell of berries from her shampoo still lingers somewhere on me, as I catch random whiffs when I move. I don't know when I realized it, but I know that I want her. I want Alexandra Seth to be mine.

While I shower, I remember that something has been on my mind since I heard the news about the fire at Alexandra's lab. I know there is a possibility that someone from my company is the mastermind behind the destruction, but I am also certain that there has to be an inside man or woman. Someone has betrayed her, and it is important to me to find out who.

Selfishly, I want her to know that she can trust herself and the belief she has in me. But, also for retribution on Alexandra's behalf for all the pain I put her through.

After my shower and getting dressed, I reach for my phone and call a private investigator that my company has used in the past.

"This is Ellis Brent. I need you to look into something for me. Do you have time for a new case?" I speak into my phone.

"Yes. For you. Always." I hear over the line.

"Great. I'll forward you the details along with your retainer. Per usual, be discreet and quick."

"When am I never?" My P.I. answers. And that is enough for me. I text him basic details of what I am looking for, knowing that he will find something if there is something to be found. I know it in my gut.

I take a deep breath as I glance out the window. The sky is transitioning from orange to blue, as the sun is rising from the horizon. The side of my mouth curves into a smile as I remember Alexandra in her doorway last night, asking me to join her inside. I head to the kitchen to put a pod in the coffeemaker.

As the machine brews coffee into my mug, I think about the night we just spent together—the smell of alcohol on her breath, the taste of her mouth, the sounds of her moans. I catch myself gripping the edge of the counter just thinking about her. My throat is starting to get dry again. Alexandra was wilder than I expected last night.

Just thinking about her is enough to make blood start rushing to my groin. The coffee machine stops whirring and I yank myself back to reality.

I need to get back to the office. See if there's anything I can find out there. Grabbing everything I need for the day, I head out to my car and drive to the Brent-Sigma office.

"Can I get a note card and envelope?" I ask my secretary when I walk up to my office.

She hands them to me, and I find a pen on her desk to write in the card.

Alexandra, thank you for talking with me last night.
I'm giving you all the space you need, but just know
that I'm sorry for hurting you. Love, Ellis

As I write *Love, Ellis*, it crosses my mind that she could think that "Love" is a presumptuous word. But I go ahead and write it, in place of "From", as it is more sincere and conveys my true feelings. I'm hopeful that she might not think of me as an enemy any longer.

I place the notecard in the envelope and seal it. Asking my secretary, "Please order the kind of flowers that say, 'I'm sorry', and send them to Alexandra Seth. Thank you, Cynthia."

Then, I head into my office.

Sitting at my desk, I type in a search for Seth BioTech personnel, specifically the team that works closely with Alexandra. A dozen names come up, from members of her board to the CEO she had installed two years ago, presumably because she wanted to focus on work in the laboratory. After reading through all the bios of those closest to Alexandra, I can't find anything suspicious.

My cell phone rings and a glance at the screen gives me a jump. It is my Private Investigator. I answer the call.

"That was fast," is my greeting.

My P.I. tells me how it wasn't hard to find interesting connections between someone close to Alexandra and my company. He says, "I'll keep looking for more and will get back to you if I find anything, but for now just check your email for details."

When I open up my email, as soon as I see the report I can tell that I have everything I need.

The message shows the security footage and data from Seth BioTech from the night of the fire. It has the log revealing that Tracey Devina's card was used to access the part of the building where the sprinklers could be manually turned off. Security cameras also recorded her in the security guard's booth while he was away from his post.

I lean forward in my reclining chair with renewed interest in all of the information. There has to be more damning evidence than some video and ID card swipes.

"Tracey Devina," I mutter to myself as I switch tabs in my Internet program back to the Seth BioTech personnel page that I was looking at when my P.I. called.

Tracey is Alexandra's lab assistant, I notice, looking at her employee headshot on my screen.

She was hired about four years ago and according to the reports by the fire master, she was the last person in the lab before the fire started.

The information in the report then reveals exactly what I need to present to Alexandra. Tracey's mother's name is Caroline Wells. She was a pharmaceutical rep at Brent-Sigma for 16 years until just under five years ago when she went on medical leave.

I minimize the Internet program and switched to the Brent-Sigma database of employees. In her personnel file, I was only able to find that Caroline Wells left on medical leave. The notes show that after claiming all of her available benefits, she resigned for medical reasons.

Continuing with the report, I read that Caroline participated in Seth BioTech clinical trials for a cancer therapy and she is still alive today. In addition, there were suspicious payments made to completely cover all of Caroline Wells' medical bills, exactly one week before Tracey Devina started working at Seth BioTech. In the email message, my P.I. mentions that he is positive that he can track the money trail, but that I have enough evidence to show that Tracey Devina took money to pay for her mother's medical bills in exchange for being an insider at Seth BioTech.

I return to Tracey's profile and study the look on her face. There is something about her and her story that still doesn't sit well with me. However, I have enough information to pass on to Alexandra.

I have to call her, I think to myself, picking up my cell phone.

When Alexandra picks up, I can tell that she is upset. "Hey." My voice tentative, unsure of what to expect. "What is it? What's wrong?"

"It was Tracey." She cries. "She sabotaged the lab. How did I not see this?"

I stand up from my seat, not sure of what to say to her after learning that she already knows the truth. Just one day after finding out about me, she is finding out that her lab assistant, whom she had worked most closely with for the past four years, is behind the fire that threatened to destroy her life's work.

Alexandra tells me that she found out about Tracey and the fire through the security footage.

"I'm so sorry," I tell her, stumbling upon the right words to say in concern and unsure when the right time is to share what I discovered.

"You don't sound surprised," she realizes. "Why don't you sound surprised?" Her voice sounds like she is saying *if there is something I don't know, you better tell me now.*

Releasing a deep sigh, I tell her everything my private investigator revealed to me.

I explain to her that I still believe there is something more to it—I still believe that Tracey Devina is a cog in a very large machine.

"My private investigator is looking for more, including the money trail." When I tell her about Tracey taking money to work on the inside, I hear Alexandra gasp.

"When the police went to arrest Tracey," she explains, "They found her at her apartment with packed bags and three hundred thousand dollars in cash."

"So, for sure, Tracey Devina is just a pawn and this goes way deeper." I look up from my desk and I see Richard walk right by my office. He has a smug look on his face, like he is invincible. Our eyes meet and he gives me a slight nod as he walks by. "Alexandra, let's meet and talk in person."

"Hey, Richard!" I yell as I open my office door and walk out into the hallway, in the direction I had seen him walk. He is no longer in the hallway, so I walk to the conference room, which was the direction he was headed.

When I get there, I see that one other person was waiting for Richard's arrival. It's Belinda, the blond, curly-haired board member. They both look over at me when I enter the room.

"Ellis, son, I was just talking with Belinda about the company's next moves." Richard gestures to another a chair, offering me a seat with them at the table. I shake my head and remain standing.

"Richard, Belinda," I nod my head to each person as I say their name.

In her usual, flat voice Belinda replies to a question I didn't voice, but that I was actually thinking. "I'm focused on injecting money into new research and development and am in charge of overseeing the move in that direction."

I shake my head *yes*, to show that I agree with what she's saying. Belinda adds, "Just as you requested at the meeting yesterday."

Richard's voice booms, "Great idea son! It's exactly what our company needs. A new direction. New prospects! And speaking of new prospects, I'm setting my sights on other companies to buy. Errr, *other* companies who want to work with us."

I can't help but notice in both of their voices that they're trying to say exactly what I want to hear. So I tell them, "Thank you, to both of you, for taking charge and moving the company in this new direction. On a different note, about that fire last night at Seth BioTech…"

Belinda readily jumps in, "We've already sent a card to Seth BioTech as well as issued an announcement on our company website expressing Brent-Sigma's sympathies for that tragedy. We've issued a very large donation in Seth BioTech's name to the U.S. Cancer Foundation."

There's no way for me to determine their sincerity and I still don't trust them, but at least I know that Alexandra's company is no longer their target.

"Good work. Carry on." I nod to Richard and Belinda, then leave them together in the conference room.

***

Two weeks after Tracey Devina was arrested, Alexandra and I are still trying to figure out how deep the roots of the sabotage go. We are both running separate investigations and sharing intel, but the money trail to Tracey Devina has run cold.

I was really hoping to find connections between anyone at Brent-Sigma and the money, but my P.I. says it is as if the money just magically appeared out of thin air. There is basically no trail.

One day, I am in my office when I receive a call from a correctional facility in the Central Valley, about an hour south of Sacramento. I accept the call.

"Mr. Brent." The woman's voice is clear and almost sweet.

"Ms. Devina." I answer. Knowing who she is before she introduces herself.

"Seems like you don't need an introduction, so I'll cut to the chase. I have information that you will find…useful." My chest tightens. I knew there was something up with her confession. She had claimed to be the only one who orchestrated the sabotage, but with the medical bill payments and the lump sum of cash to leave town, it was obviously a payoff.

"What information?" I inquire. "I'm warning you Ms. Devina. Don't waste my time."

"Now, now," she tells me. "Come see me this afternoon." The call drops.

For a second, I think about calling Alexandra, but I decide instead that it will be best to go by myself then tell her later if there is any information to share. After all, she is busy getting her research back on track.

I had memorized the name of the correctional facility from when the inmate call was announced, so I grab my jacket and head down to the parking lot. I get into my car and head out of the city, to where Tracey Devina is being detained.

Inside the facility, I am brought to a visitor's room where I will speak to Tracey using a phone on the wall. A thick pane of clear fiberglass separates the visitors from the inmates. I hear the long, loud buzzing sound from the doors on the prison side before they open.

Part of me wonders if this will all be for naught, but I figure there is no going back. And I need to get to the bottom of it— all of it. If there is anything Tracey can add to the story, then I will be open to it.

Tracey walks through the door on the other side of the partition and sits in the seat opposite me. She is wearing a grey tee shirt and grey pants that are cinched at the waist. I take the phone out of its berth on the wall, and so does she.

"At first, I didn't think you had it in you to show up ... but then I remembered you were once a Marine. You must have seen way worse than a ladies' correctional facility." Her attempt at humor or a compliment pass by unappreciated.

"Why did you ask me to meet you here today?" Impatient, I don't plan to exchange small talk with her. I need answers and I don't intend to stay with her here for long.

"Hmmm." It looks like she is thinking about what she wants to say next. Like she wanted to see me face-to-face so that she can decide whether I am worthy of hearing what she has to say, and now she may not be so sure. Then she glances left and right to make sure no one else is listening in before turning back to me. She looks different from the person whose headshot I had seen on the Seth BioTech website, like a thin mask has been peeled off her demeanor.

"I need you to get me out of here," she whispers into the phone.

"Now why exactly would I do that?" I ask, almost laughing at her absurd demand. *She has to be joking.*

She chuckles. "Because my interests align with yours. Everything I did was for your benefit and that of your company."

"First of all. You needed money for your mother's medical bills, and you skimmed some for yourself. Secondly, I don't know you. And, I definitely never asked you to do anything for me." I hope I made that clear. I don't know whom she was working with, but from what she's saying, I'm guessing that she thinks whoever got her to set the lab fire had done so on my behalf.

She shoots me a look like she has made a mistake calling me in the first place. "What the hell are you talking about?" She asks me. An incredulous look spreads across her face, and it is that brief moment when I think that I notice a look of confusion or maybe it is shock. She then places the phone back in its berth and calls the guard to take her back.

Her last question sticks around and causes me confusion. *What did she mean, 'What the hell are you talking about?'* As I walk back to my car, I get the ominous feeling that none of this is even close to being finished.

Chapter Twelve

Alexandra

Thursday

When Ellis calls to tell me that he wants to meet me and talk in person, my heart races and my stomach twists in somersaults. It is a strange time for me to get the butterflies over a man, when my lab was just destroyed, and my closest co-worker was arrested for setting the fire.

I chalk it up to being overwhelmed with emotions and give myself some grace to feel whatever the hell I am going to feel.

After all, insurance will cover the construction of a new lab. Brent-Sigma will no longer be a threat since they would be the first to be suspected of shady dealings. The connection to Tracey, though circumstantial at best, would be enough to put their corporate activities under the microscope. And, I am positive that is the last thing they want.

The files that I had downloaded to an external hard drive three days earlier are instrumental in ensuring that we won't lose more than a few weeks in the research that we are doing. I can just load any data that is missing and redo the tests that were started before and destroyed in the fire.

Plus, I now have proof and know that Ellis had nothing to do with the fire. In fact, he has done everything he can to help with the investigation. And everything else he told me, besides omitting his last name for the first two days, was the truth.

"Let's meet at the coffee shop," I tell him. And about 20 minutes later, we do.

When I see him walk up, I feel giddy with how his emerald eyes shine when they look back at me. They send me a simple spark. The same spark that sent my toes curling at this same coffee shop just three days before.

I reach my hand out to him, palm up and fingers spread. An amazed look appears on his face. The look shows that he temporarily questions whether he understands my intent. But he grabs my hand, and I start walking. He follows my gait, next to me on the sidewalk.

Together, we walk and talk. First, about holding hands, walking together in public, and where our relationship will go from there. I let him know that I meant it when I said I believed his feelings for me and that I am open to seeing where it all leads. And that since he had nothing to do with the fire, there is nothing I have to forgive him for.

When I tell him that I want us to date, in the open, and without regard to who might photograph us or write an article, he is elated. I know that makes him feel as light as it makes me feel, as he takes me in his arms in the middle of the sidewalk and spins me around, kissing me with joy and exhilaration. We have nothing to hide.

I feel that it could actually strengthen my company's position for Ellis and I to be seen in public, rather than caught sneaking around. If a reporter has a question about Seth BioTech's intentions with any other company, they won't have a problem finding me and asking me directly.

Then we talk about the fire, Tracey, and his suspicions that there must be a connection somewhere within Brent-Sigma.

But, since he doesn't have proof of any connection, he can only wait until his private investigator gets back to him.

We agree that we should continue our separate investigations and that we'd keep our eyes on the lookout for other conspirators.

***

Almost two and a half weeks after the fire, Ellis informs me that Tracey called him and asked him to visit her at the place where she is being detained. He apologizes that he didn't tell me right when she called and that he went to visit her. But as it turns out, she wanted to bribe him with information in exchange for helping her to get out of prison. He says he didn't think she had anything worth hearing. So, he left her there.

In the weeks since the fire, I have been able to start my research back up at a second lab location. We temporarily moved my staff to a different building while construction is underway to rehabilitate the original offices.

A new building, housing a bigger, better lab, is under construction in the lot next door. Everything at Seth BioTech is still progressing according to schedule, and the fire has proven to be just a minor bump in the road.

Ellis and I sort of did things backwards. We started off with this intense attraction and a whirlwind of sex, lust, and desire. Now, we're dating and getting to know one another.

Don't get me wrong. We've enjoyed a lot of sex these past couple of weeks, and I admit to myself that I'm falling for the Ellis I've come to know. The Ellis that I'm going to enjoy continuing to get to know.

I've been waiting on my front porch for just a few minutes when Ellis arrives in his car to pick me up for a date. He stops his car next to the curb in front of my house and hops out.

Flashing his perfect smile and blinding me with his emerald eyes, he walks around his car and waits for me by the passenger door. I walk into his arms that he's stretched out for me, to enter his inner circle of sandalwood. *And is that rosemary?* He kisses me in greeting, and my legs might give out on me.

"So, what do you have in store for our date today?" I ask, picking a piece of lint off his chin and leaving a kiss in its place.

He pulls out a familiar book and says, "I thought we'd have a picnic and read this literary classic to one another."

"Ahh, yes. <u>Billion Dollar Baby Daddy: An Enemies to Lovers, Secret Baby, Off-Limits Romance</u>." I exclaim, reading the title of the familiar book. "A must-read for any bibliophile.

About the grumpy billionaire who falls for the brilliant scientist."

Ellis hugs me in his arms again and kisses me in a way that communicates gratitude for our date, excitement for our connection, and the passion that I know we share. When we pull away from this long and tender kiss, he whispers to me. "And he has fallen hard."

Epilogue

Tuesday

About Two Months Later

I know that by initiating this meeting with Tracey Devina that I'm taking a dangerous chance of making a mess of things, even worse than they already are.

The hair on my arms raise at attention and an uncomfortable chill snakes up my back when I step foot into the cold and unwelcoming confines of the women's detention center near Gillis, CA. I take a deep breath before I walk in. I have never been inside a prison before, and the sight of barbed wire fences looming over 20 feet above, barred walls and doors, and multiple manned checkpoints makes me feel uneasy.

But I must speak with Ms. Devina. She is the only person who knows everyone involved with the Brent-Sigma/Seth

BioTech deal and the attempt to sabotage Seth BioTech's laboratory.

My heart is pounding with anticipation and nervous energy as I enter the visiting area. A young woman with blonde hair and cold, but pretty eyes, is brought in at the same time. We sit on opposite sides of a reinforced glass partition.

When our eyes meet, I can see the weariness etched on her face. A palpable tension fills the air in the small, colorless room.

My voice trembles as I introduce myself, but I try to insert any strength I have to not give her a negative first impression. I don't want to sound too desperate and possibly spook her. It's important that she stays and talks with me so that I can understand the motives behind her crime.

"Excuse me, are you Tracey?" I ask, realizing right away that I've asked an apparent fact. The guards wouldn't have placed her in front of me if she was someone else.

I shake off my mistake and tell her my name, then continue, "I was hoping to talk to you about your case."

Tracey looks up at me, her eyes cautious. "How do you know Ellis Brent? And how are you connected to all of this? Are you a lawyer? Wait, are you getting me out of here?" She is asking me a string of questions, and I wonder if she doesn't get many visitors. She is chatty, off the bat, with someone she doesn't know. *I wonder if I'm the first person to visit her. Has she just been dropped off in jail and forgotten about?*

"I'm not a lawyer." Tracey's eyes drop and she slouches in her chair when she hears this statement. "But if you can answer some questions for me and tell me your side of the story, then maybe we can help each other," I tell her, leaning forward in the metal chair. "I know the side of the story that I've heard in the News. I also know that you're not giving up the name of whoever paid you to commit your crimes."

Tracey hesitates for a moment, gauging whether I'm someone she should be talking to. "Why should I trust you?" she asks, her voice flat. "I did what I had to do to help my mother get out from under her mountain of debt, and to get her into the Seth BioTech immunotherapy trials. She's alive and healthy today. For me, that's all that matters. Since I'm already convicted and serving my time, I can say all that."

I nod, knowing that there is more to the story. Obviously, she loves her mother and it's my guess that at her core, Tracey Devina is not a bad person. *She did really bad things for a good reason. But, instead of whoever paid her to do these bad things, she's the only one paying for it with her freedom.*

"I understand that it can be hard to talk about, and I also get why you should be afraid." I am trying to speak with her in a gentle, caring voice so that I don't scare her, but also so she might feel comfortable with me. "The people on the other side of the money are rich and powerful."

Tracey studies my expression and takes her time to assess the man sitting before her. "Let's cut to the chase," she says, then hesitantly adds, "I am getting that you understand the deal I made. But what's in it for you?"

Sitting across from Tracey, I can sense the weight of her despair. She looks fragile, her eyes are fighting back tears. I also sense Hope. The hope that someone might be able to help her. That someone might *want* to help her.

"Before I answer that for you. Tell me your thoughts about Alexandra Seth." I am still trying to sound steady and kind so that she might come to trust me. However, she still doesn't know whose side I'm on. So, I also need to seem unbiased until I can figure out where her loyalties lie.

Tracey adjusts in her chair, then starts to answer my question. "Alexandra is focused and ambitious. She's determined and brilliant. Our relationship was purely professional. She was never a friend, and we didn't do things together socially. We saw one another every day for almost four years and not once did she ask me about my life." Tracey's face remains the same throughout her account.

She pauses a moment, but I remain quiet. Then she continues, "When I first started, I tried to ask her questions about her family or find out if she was in a relationship, but she quickly redirected our conversation. From my first month of working with Alexandra, she made it clear that the research was our only focus. Not even small talk."

"When Alexandra showed up after the fire, the first thing she did was find me and hug me." Tracey wipes away tears that she could not hold back.

"That hug. It really surprised me. Hold on, I'm sorry." She is unable to continue speaking and pulls the bottom hem of her shirt up in order to dig her face in and allow herself to freely sob.

My own feelings of sympathy and pity well up for her. I gather that what she is showing me is sincere, and not an act. But, I also think that this is the time, while her vulnerability is splayed wide open, and she's possibly feeling like whoever hired her is just going to let her sit and rot in jail, that she might be desperate enough for anyone's help. Even mine. A stranger to her. But someone, at least, who is physically sitting in front of her, wanting some information that couldn't make anything worse. But could potentially make things better.

When she's able to collect herself, she says, "Alexandra asked me how I was and told me she was just relieved that I wasn't hurt and that no one else was either. That was her number one concern. It was only after everyone assured her that there were no injuries or worse did she ask me about the lab and our... I mean, her research."

Tracey is still attempting to get through what she's trying to tell me, through sobs and chokes as she recalls her encounter with Alexandra the night of the fire.

She struggles through a gulp and says, "With the previous four years of the research being the only focus, it wasn't hard to be an insider, to get information about the research and the company. She wasn't my friend. She didn't care about me, so I didn't care about her."

Tracey raises her eyes to mine, then she continues. Her cheeks are wet with tears, her face red, and her eyes puffy. "However, she did care about me. She cared about everyone. When it mattered. But all this time that should have been evident to me, because at the root of it all, that's the reason for the research. It's for everyone. Her research will benefit everyone. How was I? How? How could I be so stupid!? I cared about the research too. That's what I went to school to do. What Alexandra and I were doing was important. It meant something. To millions of people! But, I only realize that now that it's too late. Now, I can only sit in this place every single day and wonder, was it all worth it? Could I have helped my mom without having to do all these awful things to Alexandra and her research!?" Again, she buries her face in the hem of her shirt and sobs.

I let her sit and cry for a bit, but then look at my watch and see that we only have two more minutes left in our visit.

"Tracey," I say, wishing that I didn't have to interrupt her outpouring of emotion. She looks up and I point to the clock on the wall behind me. She understands my meaning. We don't have much time together.

With eyes that I hope show concern and understanding for the choices that she felt she had to make, I tell her, "I think you obviously feel bad for what you did and you were stuck making an impossible decision. But, to make things right. Whether that means you can get out of here or just make sure that justice is served, please tell me. Who paid you to do all this? Who is behind all of it?"

Her lips open then close, the inner dialogue apparent on her face. With another look up at the clock and her voice trembling with emotion, she speaks the name, "Richard Cross."

The name that Tracey spoke hangs in the rafters of my mind well after I leave the detention center. She said there was no one else, even when I asked her if she was absolutely sure.

But, I already knew that Richard Cross played a part. I'm the one who planted the seed in his mind to get Tracey to set fire to Alexandra's lab.

What I wanted her to tell me was how Ellis Brent was involved.

Brent-Sigma has bought into and broken up dozens of other companies, but when I found out that its next target was Seth BioTech, there was no way I would stand back and allow that to happen.

I know that Ellis had only been CEO at Brent-Sigma for a month, but he must have been integral to his company's attempt to buy into Seth BioTech. There's no way he wasn't involved.

I have made too many sacrifices and have suffered too much loss, and now that Ellis and Alexandra are in a relationship...

When I get back to my car, I reach for the letter that I had started to write to Alexandra. Finding a pen in the middle console, I write the final two paragraphs.

Tracey Devina did not work alone. Brent-Sigma and the drugs they create are the real criminals here, robbing people of their health, their dignity, and their lives. I hope we can meet and catch up. After all this time.

The evening sun is beating down into my car, directly in my eyes. So I reach up to pull down the visor to block some of the bright light. Clipped into the flap is my favorite photograph. Her beautiful face on an equally beautiful sunny day.

Dark, wavy hair flows to her shoulders, framing a smile reserved just for me. Her expressive grey eyes reach back at me adoringly and with a playful mischief, saying, *Not another photo, you stinker. I'll get you!*

My heart fills with the all-encompassing warmth of devotion and love, then with the hollow pangs of loss and remembrance. It's these feelings that have led me to do everything I had to do. Right now, Alexandra might think that whoever is behind the fire is her enemy. But, I can help her understand that it was all to help her.

I look back down to the letter I'm writing, wanting to finish it so that I can send it off.

> *I hope we can get together to catch up and I can tell*
> *you more about where I've been and why I had to*
> *stay away. Please call me, I've written my number*
> *below. I love you, Bug.*
>
> *Love, Dad*

I slide the letter into the envelope and seal it, sticking a stamp in the corner. Then I start the car and drive off toward the post office.

Tell Me the Truth

Sofie Daves

Author Bio

My life used to circle around my three kids' schools, sports, and activities. Now that they're older and don't need me to bring snacks after the game, I've decided to take the next logical step … write steamy romance novels.

I love game nights, Happy Hour, book club, running, paddle boarding, and hiking near home in the Sierra Nevada foothills, California. I probably drink more than I should, enjoy too much time with girlfriends, and over-indulge in "ME" time. But, I'm lucky that the LOVE of my life for over 30 years sticks around and my kids still call me Momma. Oh, and my dogs love me!

Learn more at SofieDaves.com

Sofie Daves

Authors Note

Thank you for reading my first published, full-length novel. When I started writing about Ellis and Alexandra, I fell in love with them and have been able to write their story in three stand-alone books.

If you haven't yet had the chance to read the prequel novella in this series, <u>Love, the Enemy</u>, please visit my website where you can join my mailing list and download it for free.

You'll also receive updates on all my new releases, deals, recommended reads, and more!

Now I'm off to finish my next book, which I have scheduled for release on July 1st, 2023!

~Love, Sofie

www.SofieDaves.com
www.facebook.com/SofieDaves
www.amazon.com/author/sofiedaves
https://www.goodreads.com/SofieDaves

Sofie Daves

Sneak Peek

Untitled Release

July 1st, 2023

After an incredibly busy day at the bakery, utterly exhausted, I finally return home with one goal in mind: to relax with Theo, go to bed early, and sleep like a log. I'm so tired that I might let Theo have sex with me, but only if I don't have to move.

As I step inside my apartment, the warm scent of burning candles greets me. They provide the only light in a room hushed with darkness.

"Oh, no," I whisper to myself, feeling a sinking realization. The chaotic rush of customers at the bakery had completely made me forget to bring a gift home to Theo for Valentine's Day.

The candlelight and floating aroma of vanilla, rosemary, lavender, and lasagna create a cozy and inviting ambiance. On the dining room table, I can see that Theo has set out a bottle of Zinfandel that I'm pretty sure we picked out together when we were out wine-tasting a month ago.

I hear Theo singing to himself while preparing his favorite lasagna. Taking advantage of the moment, I quietly slip into the bedroom, hoping that he doesn't notice.

I feel a pang of guilt for not having anything to give him tonight, especially since it seems like he has put in a lot of effort to create a special evening. I put on a beautiful black dress that accentuates my curves, but then think of what I can give him instead of this dress for the perfect Valentine's gift.

When I emerge from the bedroom, I have let my hair down loose from its bun and am wearing a black mesh negligee with creatively placed lace details and black stilettos. Walking into the living room, I can't help but feel a bit embarrassed at the state of my messy apartment, however, Theo went above and beyond my expectations, transforming it the best he could into a truly enchanting space.

Theo is standing by the dining room table dressed in tan pants, a crisp white shirt, and a navy-blue blazer. When he sees me, I notice a flicker of appreciation display across his face.

As I walk over to him, I'm taking in the scene he has carefully crafted. The table is adorned with flickering candles, casting a warm and romantic glow throughout the rooms. The air is filled with the scent of candles and the irresistible aroma of lasagna and freshly tossed salad, making my stomach rumble with hunger.

"I'm suddenly not feeling like lasagna," Theo remarks as he grins and mischievously licks his lips. He moves from around the table and stops at arm's length, taking both of my hands in his and stretching them out to the left and right, allowing him a full view of my scantily clad body.

"Hmmm, mmmm!" He hums as he releases my hands and pulls me in close for a kiss. Our tongues play a push-and-pull game, bringing us further into one another.

I can feel his excitement in his kiss, the thump of his heart in his chest through his shirt, as well as the hardness on my hip, coming through from the front of his pants.

"Do you want what I got you for Valentine's Day?" I ask as I pull just far enough away from his kiss so that I can speak.

I've obviously just gotten a second wind. I then reach back to bite his bottom lip softly between the front of my teeth.

***

"You can put your pants back on, but leave your tie, please," I tell Theo after he's had his way with me, having leaned me over the dining room table and finishing me off against the wall.

I have taken my seat at the table, hungry. And, not wasting time to put back on my flimsy piece of mesh and lace, that is basically the equivalent of being naked anyway.

Theo delicately arranged the salad in a bowl that I remember as being special. We picked the bowl up last month when we were out wine tasting in the Amador Valley and shopping in Sutter Creek. He serves a hefty serving of salad onto my plate, then serves a smaller portion for himself. I can appreciate that he knows that I prefer three-quarters of my plate to be vegetables and only a quarter of it anything else.

While we are talking and eating our salads, I can see a mix of excitement and nervousness on his face and in his voice. He has planned this surprise Valentine's Day dinner to show me just how much he cares. I silently hope to myself that my little present was enough to match the effort he's made this evening to make it truly memorable.

"Thank you for all of this, Theo," I tell him as I wave my hand around to show him I mean the dinner and all he did in my apartment to set the mood. "I'm sorry I didn't get you a gift." With a coy smile, I play at being fully apologetic. But I know he's perfectly happy with the present he just received as well as the gift of me sitting naked next to him at the table.

He chuckles, and his touch gently caresses my cheek. "You being here, looking like a vision, is more than I ever will want. And, there are plenty more surprises in store for tonight, which I have a feeling you're going to love."

"Happy Valentine's Day, my love," Theo's voice fills the room and the happiness I feel explodes into a million starbursts.

A sweet smile graces my face as I reply, "Happy Valentine's Day to you too, babe." And I lean over to give him a kiss.

He then gestures toward the wine, silently inviting us to indulge. I nod, feeling grateful for this special moment with him. As we savor our meal, we share stories from our day, cherishing the simple joy of being together. It dawns on me that Theo has devoted the entire day to creating this perfect evening, and my heart swells with appreciation.

His words carry deep meaning, expressing his gratitude for our relationship and the love we share. A flutter of excitement stirs within me, as I sense something more significant unfolding. He is about to propose.

Nervousness tinges on my thoughts, reminding me that I'm still unsure of how to respond to such a life-changing question. I didn't have time to stop to think about how I would respond if he asked me to marry him. What will I say? How do I think about the whole thing? Am I ready to be engaged?

"Excuse me for a moment," I murmur, excusing myself to go to the bathroom.

Gazing at my reflection in the mirror, I see a beautiful, accomplished woman ready to embrace what lay ahead. Amidst the whirlwind of emotions, I remind myself of the journey that led me here—the sacrifices I made and the dreams I pursued.

Plus, I have great boobs. I look at my bare boobs in the mirror and chuckle to myself that I'm just walking around naked with Theo and it's so comfortable and seems totally natural.

Confidence fills my heart as I whisper words of encouragement. Olivia, you've come so far, worked so hard. Perhaps it's time to embrace the next chapter of your life. But remember, it's your decision, and it's essential to approach it with clarity and self-love. Trust yourself, Olivia. With renewed determination, I take in a deep breath and return to the living room, ready to face the future hand-in-hand with Theo.

As I take my seat next to him again, our gazes lock. It seems that Theo can't help but express his feelings.

"Liv, these past six months with you have been the best six months of my life. You've brought so much love, joy, and laughter into my world. I can't begin to express how much you mean to me and how much I cherish you." He swings his knees toward me and adjusts himself in his chair. "Your presence in my life has ignited a fire within me, a flame that burns brighter with each passing day. Olivia, you have brought the kind of life into my world that I never knew existed. Your laughter, and your smile, fill me with indescribable joy. You are the light in my darkest moments, the rock that holds me steady. I consider myself the luckiest person on this planet to have you by my side." Theo pauses to see my reaction to the expression of his feelings.

Touched by his words, I reach over to hold his hand. He smiles tenderly, his eyes shining with adoration.

"You are my inspiration, my motivation, and my heart's greatest desire. Olivia, my love for you knows no bounds. It transcends time and space. With you, every moment is an eternity, and every touch is an electric shock that resonates through my entire being. You have become the best thing that has ever happened to me, and I am eternally grateful for your love," he continues.

Blushing, I lower my gaze briefly before meeting his eyes again.

Theo stands up from his chair, and reaches into his pocket, retrieving a small, velvet box. He then gets down on one knee as I fully turn to face him, still sitting in my chair. When he speaks again, his voice is trembling with emotion. "Liv, my love for you will only grow stronger with each passing day. I promise to cherish and adore you for the rest of my life. I want to spend the rest of my life with you. Will you marry me, Olivia Whitman?"

I didn't know that Theo could be such a romantic. Every word he spoke sounded like something out of a book but I can see the sincerity in his eyes and they are telling me that he means every word he is saying.

My eyes widen, and my breath is catching in my throat. I had had my doubts about marriage, but at that moment, all my doubts have vanished. The love and certainty shining in Theo's eyes are all I need to know.

"Theo, I can't wait to see what the future holds for us. So, yes!" I say as he slips a beautiful diamond ring on my left ring finger and I lean over to wrap my arms around his neck. "Yes, I will marry you, Theo Stone!"

Ecstatic, Theo leans forward, capturing my lips as we come together in a passionate kiss. We are savoring the moment, with our love and excitement intertwining. I am already naked and can feel that he's ready for round two of dinner sex.

As I'm unbuttoning his pants, the sound of the doorbell rings through the apartment, interrupting our blissful bubble. Theo sighs, breaking the kiss reluctantly and redoing the button on his pants.

***

"You son of a bitch!" Theo's voice echoes through the doorway as he opens the front door.

A husky voice responds, "Good to see you too."

"You were supposed to come tomorrow," Theo exclaims, his tone filled with surprise.

"I thought I'd surprise you. Is this not a good time?" the man asks.

"No, no. It's completely fine. Come right in," Theo replies, inviting the man inside.

Unfamiliar with the guest's voice, I realize this isn't an ideal moment for an unexpected visit. I most certainly am not dressed to welcome guests. I'm not even dressed.

I hurry and retreat to my bedroom to change into something more presentable. Namely, clothes. Ha ha. While I am choosing what to wear, laughter fills the living room. He and his new guest sound like they're wrestling because I can hear some shuffling and grunts on the other side of my bedroom door.

Something falls, then a "Hey watch out! Liv will be so pissed!" More shuffling and bang! "Ow, you asshole! Come 'ere!" Then some muffled sounds and an "OK! Uncle! Uncle!" Out of Theo.

I throw on a casual dress and step into the living room, curious to meet the person who is now in my apartment and has apparently awakened Theo's inner child. The boys have resumed their wrestling and it really is cute to see Theo acting like a thirteen-year-old boy, rolling around mostly on the sofa, partially on the ground and in mid-air. Both men laughing the whole time.

Theo is now on top of his friend, while his friend is face-down, apparently trying to regain dominance. It takes Theo a few moments to look up and notice me standing there, watching.

"Oh, there she is! The love of my life!" He exclaims while keeping his hand pressed down on his shoulder, not letting his friend get up just yet. "Oh you can't, can you? What's wrong huh? What's up? Not you!"

Theo's friend shows some incredible strength and is somehow able to lift a few inches off the ground, with Theo still on top of him. Theo crawls off of his friend, then childishly pushes his friend's head down once more while standing up for playful emphasis. Theo walks over to me enthusiastically, and his friend grabs his leg, tripping Theo and making him fall down at my feet.

Theo yells back, "Asshole, I said here she is! Get up and meet my fiancé!" He then stands up next to me, moving his hand behind my back to encourage me to walk over to meet his friend who is also getting up from his previous position. "Come on, Liv. This is Nico. He's a day early, but that's just who he is."

Nico? So this is THE Nico, Theo's childhood friend that he can't stop talking about? Interested, I step forward and reach out my hand, saying, "Theo is always mentioning Nico this, and Nico that. It's nice to finally meet you."

"Likewise," Nico replies, finally standing up and looking up at me, his face finally in view.

As soon as I see his face, I feel a mixture of horror and shock but do my best not to let these feelings fill my eyes. But my expression must be ghastly, as a whirlwind of emotion paints my skin in a myriad of colors. A lump forms in my throat, as if the ground has been pulled from beneath my feet. The serenity I had felt just moments ago seems poised to shatter. I am trying not to overreact.

To my astonishment, Nico is none other than Dominic—the man I had shared a passionate one-night stand with two years ago.

Tell Me the Truth

www.SofieDaves.com

www.facebook.com/SofieDaves

www.amazon.com/author/sofiedaves

https://www.goodreads.com/SofieDaves

Printed in Great Britain
by Amazon